A dark, gleaming jewel of a novel with dramatic echoes of Beckett and Dickens, about the harrowing life of a fourteen-year-old, virtually homeless boy growing up at the extreme edge of poverty and emotional deprivation. With the drug and illegal gun-sale world of South Dallas as a sharply delineated backdrop, this beautifully written first novel power-fully and unsentimentally describes, in crystalline prose, the costs of a no-childhood childhood.

Lis Harris, Columbia University, former *New Yorker* staff writer, author of *Holy Days* and *Rules of Engagement*

City Limit is an intense, gritty novel of a bleak, hopeless urban landscape, unrelenting and remorse-less. Told in a matter of fact, black and white documentary film-like narrative, unembellished by literary conceits, and all the more dark for it, the book depicts the life of a fourteen-year-old child living on the streets of a decrepit area in Dallas, and surviving by living in condemned buildings, selling drugs and guns, and constantly vigilant to avoid victimization. There are shades of Studs Lonegan in the story —but Miller's protagonist is strictly solitary, devoid even of the pseudo-sociality of gang membership— and an atmosphere reminiscent of Mad Max —but without the melodrama. What haunts the reader is that the story is a slice of life, replicated endlessly, absent even a spark of hope. This is a memorable, indeed haunting book that leaves the reader stunned and saddened without any use of cheap sentimentalism. Miller is a brilliant writer, as much so for what he leaves out as for what he puts in. It is a book I will not easily forget. I look forward to his future works.

Bernard E. Rollin, author of *The Unheeded Cry* and *The Frankenstein Syndrome,* University Distinguished Professor, Colorado State University

Amidst an urban jungle plagued by drugs, guns, fear, murder and poverty, a precocious youngster finds love during his daily and nightly quest for survival. Moments of happiness ensue before tragedy strikes. Pulling himself from the stranglehold of his past, he finds redemption and rebirth during the reunion with his father. It flows like a movie script and rakes the soul.

Carlos Castro Perelman, physicist, co-author of *Against the Tide*

Without fanfare this novel draws you into the head of a man-child. Chabney doesn't know he is speaking in trains of metaphors and might not even know what a metaphor is, but he turns the perfunctory English he has grown up with into a vehicle for communicating loss, conscience, disgust with the adult world, and then impatience with his own disgust.

Chabney is resourceful and industrious; one thing that makes this novel stand out is its respect for work and working. Miller attends to gun repair and illegal gun sale, and Chabney's moral rise proves that the work is worthy of such close attention.

Nicholas Pappas, author of *The Nietzsche Disappointment*, Professor of Philosophy, City University of New York

City Limit

a novel

Lantzey Miller

cover painting by Jim Bratone

ISBN-13: 978-0-9824087-2-8
ISBN-10: 0-9824087-2-2

GrandViaduct

Dallas Colorado Springs   GrandViaduct.com

To E.C.L.,

   who first listened and let it happen;

and to J.B.,

   who first insisted and made it happen.

I.

1.

I walked out on Dad one soggy night seven years ago. He was an all right guy, but he confused our apartment entry codes to the point he endangered lives.

The fact is, three years after I first left the place, the cops flattened our block, so you have to rely on my memory here. I can only hope Dad was out when the bulldozers arrived to squeeze out the bone heads. A few weeks before that invasion, the city had leveled the abandoned strip mall across Spanish Fort Avenue. Too many crackerjacks had been cooking their pebbles in the hollow storefronts. At night we used to see their lighter flares. Then the city wrapped our apartment complex in chainlink, with warning signs. Next it was a meadow of Johnson grass.

Our complex was a scatter of about thirty quadruplexes, units we called them. I believe they were the first apartments Dallas built for poor folk, to keep you there, way back in the fifties. A unit had yellow brick on the first floor, asbestos siding on the second. Through the front door, the reek of melted cheese, ammonia and diapers greeted you. A flight of stairs dropped to the basement. Over our basement stairs Dad had placed his steel door that lay horizontal over them. He'd made it when he worked at the airplane hangar. We pushed it open from below with a pole. We lived down there too, and no one lived in the apartments above.

The city was supposed to manage the complex, but the most we spotted was a blue city car crawling down Illinois

Avenue every couple months. A citizen of sorts, Rick Ocotillo, actually ran the place, with some lofty ideals. He provided free rent and safety the cops could not. The hitch was you had to buy from him. He said he sold cheap and the residents were on the kokomo anyway so he offered a true service. I met him many times in our basement, a heavy man, trim mustache, always in a gray suit and no tie. "Hey, it's the round dude," he said all happy when he came in and saw me. As if I was rounder than him. Folks called him The Face, I think because he had so much of one. He brought me model train magazines. "Great hobby for a boy," he said. "Try it." I thanked him anyway.

Dad provided him services. That is Dad provided residents with hand-held protection, which The Face required. It helped them feel safe, it kept them to the end. Business was brisk since residents turned over fast, often by surprise in the night. Many were relocated to Laurel Land's rolling green hills, down off south Lancaster.

The first floor was our buffer zone for transacting. Customers knocked on the upstairs door outside. Here's where Dad employed his entry codes.

They were a series of long and short pauses between knocks, like Morse Code. Always $- \cdot - - \cdot$ came first, for our last name, Gullo, then came the date by $-$ and $\cdot$ like binary. So February 1, 2001 would be 211, or $- \cdot \cdot - \cdot -$. Then came a tag, a series of eight $-$'s and $\cdot$'s. One string of code could be twenty or more taps. And a customer had to tap the whole code three times; two out of three knocked right got Dad reaching for the pole. The customer needed a lot of determination to get that far. Dad went up and transacted. Folks took whatever he offered.

He had Rick Ocotillo pass the entry code to customers. Dad revised it every three days, because you never knew when someone might change. "Even Rick Ocotillo," Dad said. Not counting the date, it was the tag that Dad revised, and that's where I had differences with him.

Trouble was, Dad could be sloppy. He could do too much bone, which has no place in gun dealing. He cooked his stuff in the morning with a butane torch, a .45 shell and needle nose pliers. The city had cut off the gas to the complex long as I can recall. Anybody who cooked hauled in butane. After his morning kokomo, Dad jittered foot to foot as he torched up pork chops before his appetite died for the day. When I was four he still could stand a beer can on his belly, but after years of jittering his thighs had shrunk to scissors way back in his pants. He jittered when selling a sawed-off or Colt. He made people antsy, so they took the first price he named. In that way kokomo worked for him. But it did not work for his codes.

Normally he changed the tag by leapfrogging a dot and dash. So $\cdots ----$ went to $\cdots - \cdot ---$. But he started confusing which digit leaped. He refused to write down the code in case the paper blew upstairs to the wrong feet. No use reminding him that The Face had the code on a paper scrap and copied it for our customers. I said, "It was the second dot moved, because it was January 20th , a 2 for 'second' and 0 for 'dot.'"

"Never trust a 13-year-old," he said. "That's the bad-luck age."

Then another knock came, with the third dot moved. His tiny eyes shifted to me. He jittered in place, let the three repetitions pass and lost the sale. He was losing Rick Ocotillo's cut too.

But next visit, The Face only said, "You keep depriving me my pay-per-view money, Gullo. Sell the next guy two pieces." I guessed Rick Ocotillo would have a hard time replacing Dad.

2.

The morning before I walked out, Dad and I got up to go take care of the other half of business, acquisition.

I fell into my Coogis that could fit about two of him in one leg. He made my breakfast, that is mixed the dried milk for my box of Cocoa Krispies, no complaints about my appetite. He was very polite to me, never used the f word except when trimming the white off raw pork: "I hate fat, too slimy."

We trod up through the steel hatch and to the '78 Honda. Dad drove a rusted tin can that thieves couldn't see and piloted with his cell at ear. It was an overcast February Sunday looking for its chance to dump on us. We stopped by the "High Hat" apartments off Corinth much like ours. He always called them wrong, "High Hat," saying "Hat" instead of the real word, like a dig at the residents' condition, as if they didn't mirror his own. It's one of those wrong names that sticks. In an old Baptist Sunday tradition, boneheads of South Dallas stay in bed especially late, telling themselves how this morning they'll just have to sleep through church for a change. Doors opened on droopy-eyed crackerjacks.

But they went and pried the lids off their cartons chock with metal. Screws were missing from trigger mechanisms, springs uncoiled from cartridge chambers: the usual. Dad bought the lot cheaper than the gram of hamburger helper he took too.

We puttered past the woods in the Trinity riverbottoms, and next to them the shacks of the alphabet avenues. A routine day of acquisition, I go into a daze. We used to make these rounds nighttimes, but he started getting too nervous about himself to stick his nose outside after sundown. Buying weaponry was not easy to do mornings since most of our sources kept afternoon crackerjack hours. Sure Dad was a crackerjack, but the fear of going boubou-less pushed him out of bed.

Back when I was a kid I could sneak out on him, mornings. I'd walk to William Brown Miller Elementary around the corner. The kids were about all black and I was the roly-poly Mexican though I don't believe Dad and I were Mexican. He was the one signed me up in the first place but soon appeared to forget that fact. He'd catch me coming home afternoons. "Too risky a time in this neighborhood," he said. "I'm a responsible parent." In fourth grade he started waking at eight and kept me home to work with him. I learned enough stuff by reading gun-repair manuals and the hundreds of magazines he dug from the trashes.

Stuff like the fact the worst grade for dropout rates up in Massachusetts is not fourth but eleventh, over 4%. And the vocational school rate's not so bad, 2.9%—couldn't be, if he of all folks made it through, here in Dallas. And aircraft engine mechanics like he once was can make a pretty 48 grande (I spell that right, "grande"? I can't smell it.)

About eleven o'clock this Sunday morning, Dad got a callback from Tim Stevens for five sawed-off .410's. A callback was when you were supposed to make a deal yesterday and suddenly someone's calling saying goods are in. Dad turned down callbacks since they made for ambushes. But he worked with Tim Stevens enough to trust him. "Trust, my last bad habit," Dad told me. Tim Stevens had left the stash at his grandmother's in Waxahachie, and his youngest sister Gawene was driving it in. So we had to ring his bell again today.

The screen door shed paint flecks as we waited. Tim Stevens finally opened and asked us in for coffee and lemon chiffon pie his white sister Palla served. The man was long and deep black and stooped over like a grandfolk himself. His old house reeked of mothballs and bacon grease and the ivory lace curtains were yellow. A baby slept in a wooden crate. Many crackerjacks, you find, have babies. Gawene was on her way from Waxahachie this minute. We waited out that minute through two whole pans of lemon chiffon. I could wait out many cuts of pie for Gawene and her spill of tootsie-roll hair.

Dad said, "Trouble is, I'm eating up my profits lounging here." Like he was competing with Mr. Smith-&-Wesson himself. He just hated sitting and had already had his daily meal. And hated one son's over-respecting someone's youngest sister. So he arranged for Tim Stevens to come to our place on Illinois this afternoon. Made Tim memorize the code right there. The long man rolled his eyes, trying to get that code down.

We drove a quick circuit of cracker shacks, and we sold, for ten times what he'd paid, those old guns I'd fixed with pennies' worth of parts. Half rich, we hung by the Cedar Crest Safeway for items we could store dry since we had no electricity. Beef jerky, pork skins, potato flakes. If we had made an extra large killing, we'd trust ourselves to spaghetti and clams at the Olive Garden. But not today, with acquisition half-done. We then swung by the Mesquite flea market to scrounge for pins, bushings, swivels, bolt blanks, forend screws, bands, any metal bit that could have been from a gun, for our tackle box.

We got home by 3 P.M. Rain was picking up. Illinois Avenue gick monsters were just stirring from bed. A couple dudes, too chesty to be long friends of kokomo, stood under the eaves near our door, like they planned to share our profits. Still they weren't beamed up yet, so fingers would be too shaky to handle any protection. But as Dad hustled me from the car, I felt his nerves twitching. The boubou brain, he always forgot to pack anything loaded.

Then a few units away, Rick Ocotillo made a rare outdoor appearance. He waved like he wanted to talk. Dad told me, "Afternoon around here, we'll stay inside and work, thank you." We slipped through the steel hatch. As Dad poled it shut, it fell the last several inches. Toes around the complex could have felt the quake.

I worked under the Coleman lantern prepping merchandise. Since I was about seven, Dad had lost his steady fine-tool fingers.

Soon, upstairs came the heavy Rick Ocotillo knock. "Someone's twisting his fourth and fifth digit in the tag," Dad said. Those fourth and fifth digits in the tag were correct, for all three repetitions. After the knocks there came a long unpleasant silence.

Dad paced, wadding pages of code ideas. We only had that camp stove, the bar stool where I sat working, and clothes and papers and magazines stacked in neat aisles in the living area. The high window had once looked onto a shaft well before he had bricked it up. He stayed warm with his bone and stove, me with my coat.

His evening stir crazies came on, and he tried sweeping the basement mold from the carpet. It still overpowered the sweet plastic cloud of this morning's kokomo and the solder under my nose. He read out loud from riddle and puzzle books. He shouted he used to repair jet engines at Dallas Love Field. He thrust his FAA license at me. That goatee and tiny face, he was the fox out of the children's books. He poured gin on top the boubou and started confusing himself with holy sorts, declaring himself Allah or Moses. Thanks to the silly water company, the sink tap worked, and he watered down his gin to stretch it out. He roared he would rain fire upon America for making money God.

Between his barks, rain tapped the brick in the former window.

Five P.M. brought the Stevenses' knock. Those soft knuckles had to be Gawene's. Gawene, at Illinois? "Everybody's switching their digits today," Dad said.

On a slip of paper I wrote a code, but going backwards, with a date tag for February 4, 2001. I showed him and asked what tomorrow's code would be. His answer switched a couple digits. "Nobody in their right mind can work with a code backward," he said. He had stated my point.

The heavy knocks returned. The Stevenses must have tracked down Rick Ocotillo. After two snubs this afternoon, a third would hurt The Face, especially with a customer watching at his side. Dad paced through four perfect repetitions of the code.

About now he recollected once again how I'd had an older sister for a couple years. It was her that somehow made him leave his Love Field job. A .38 Browning pistol I had once refreshed hung on a wall hook above the Bible. He grabbed it, opened the tool box of rounds and loaded the chamber. But only once had he ever flashed a hole in the ceiling.

"Vishnu saves His fire rain for heretics," he said.

I cringed at the manhandling of my handiwork, but I kept screwdrivering. He'd touched that .38 plenty times, but who knows when he'd jam the firing pin. Gin night happened only two or three times a week, since Dad frowned on booze.

In a few hours came a knock he approved of. He poled the steel door open, went up and dealt with a customer. I fingered some cash from his box of rounds, then snuck up the stairs.

I took the corner behind the front door. It goes into shadow at night. Dad sealed the sale, closed up and went down. I opened, entered rain and walked to Tim Stevens's.

3.

Let me backtrack to the beginning of that walk. I had never heard how I ended up living with the person at the front part of my life, that is Dad. But the person at this neck of my life will see how we got thrown together. That means you, Suds. Open this in ten and a half years, when you're of age.

The miles to Tim Stevens's didn't roll off my feet. One problem, the route you take to Tim Stevens's by car isn't the one you should hoof. A vehicle might recognize your big body in the headlights and then swerve too far. Dad had competition in the world, and I had associated with him.

By wheels, you just wind straight down Bonnie View to Morrell. On the way, Bonnie View cuts past William Brown Miller Elementary and the hilltop where you watch downtown sparkle way down by its river, then the Cedar Crest golf course. You cross wide lazy Cedar Crest Boulevard, then Morrell puts you into the Corinth St. valley and you slog up the hill, past the high-power lines and Morrell Avenue DART tram station, to Tim Stevens's. But by foot, if you want to avoid front bumpers straying into you, you hike some back trails.

Which brings up my footgear. Dad did invest in shoes. Our customers needed confidence in our product, and your body was the presentation package. Style of rusty car apparently did not play into the presentation. My one pair, black Forzieri oxfords, I shined every few nights. But Dad accused my hind paws of ballooning and bought shoes two sizes over. Try piloting over slick dark rocks in big hard leather.

City Limit

I first took the woods beside our strip mall, my old way to school. The rain had quit for the moment. Mud slopped into the oxfords. The toes gouged out the drunks' old broken glass and rotten logs they use for pillows. Dad had always pointed at their campfires far off, yellow flickers in blackness. "That's where too much wine and religion leads," he warned. Tonight I only smelled the damp ashes.

Bonnie View is just two lanes of beat-up asphalt, and I plugged across to the clump of trees behind the school. You sometimes see back there the butane lighters of third grader clucks cooking boubou. But rain scares off beamers old and young. The long backside of the school, the window blinds drawn, I got to missing the place. I could sit at a desk sniffing the crayons in my cigar box all morning. In the math workbook I'd fill in the sum blanks weeks ahead. There was a kid, Tonio, maybe a real Mexican with a lawn of black stubs on top. First grade, he walked right up to me, took me over the back chainlink, down to a creek. He dipped tadpoles out in his hands, called them sperm. He called himself a cowboy, his mother a raspberry, me an Indian. One November morning he stopped showing up. I searched the playgrounds for months. Dad said the same would happen to me.

Past the school I took the hole in the fence into the African middle class. There were separate houses with grass, mowed, even some ancient flamingos. The front bricks looked so quiet, maybe the crackerjacks to the south would pass them by. I dropped into the storm drain under Kiest Blvd. A six-year-old can stand in the tube, but I was crouching, my sides scraping the walls. Tonio would take me here, and we'd crunch the fried tortillas from the cafeteria. Even on this wet night, water in my shoes, I could taste that salty corn.

I caught up with Bonnie View again, where it had a sidewalk. The oxfords were wobbling across my feet. At the golf course the sidewalk stopped and a spike iron fence took over. Bonnie View wound into the dark trees. I tugged at the top rail under the spikes, but my feet stayed planted. Too many years, Dad's wheels took me the distances. And I liked Spaghetti-Os too much. Finally, using a roadside crate, I could just straddle two spikes. I landed on my feet and must have burst the soles and some new blisters.

And I halted. I looked awhile at the immense black field ahead. Rain flapped the cut grass blades and dripped down my belly. Dad's wad in my pocket had to be soaked. Returning the wad would not be easy. And next time Dad crawled out that steel hatch, he might walk right into The raging Face.

I had put myself outside for a night.

4.

I must have reached Tim Stevens's past ten o'clock. All the lights glowed. I collapsed on his covered porch so hard the bulb above the door flickered. Lying on my stomach I peeked around my body at my number-one assets, the Forzieris. The left one showed a split seam under its mud coat. The feet themselves had stopped speaking to me.

Gawene Stevens swept open the curtain of the door window and cupped hands on the glass. I raised a hand. She called to folks behind to cover her, and the door opened with a whine. But she stayed inside the screen, as if it would stop bullets. "That you, Chabney? You come to worship my porch?"

Out there somewhere the rain pattered the bushes.

I roused sometime later on a couch with three tall folks watching me from another sofa. Gray fog hung from the ceiling, smelling of burnt sugar and plastic. The baby had its head in Palla's open blouse. Its feet swam a lazy backstroke. Flanking her sat Tim Stevens and Gawene. Hers and Palla's knees in their hose were bony as Dad's. I wondered if that baby was getting any sustenance under there. At least he wasn't puling his eyes out like your average boubou baby. Both Tim's hands were gloved in bandages. "Sorry I was late coming back from Waxahachie," Gawene was saying at me. "Grandmom made me pin up the laundry before she'd fetch the goods."

The coffee table showed off a carburetor and a kabuki. Hand-painted sunflowers sagged out of the kabuki's rum bottle.

"You know Tim and Wene drove over and banged y'all's door all afternoon with that damn code," Palla said. I knew it, I would know Gawene's knuckle on my door.

"I told you all they'd be out," Gawene told her. "Sunday's busy in their business."

"Who'd you expect Tim to sell those guns to, after he went to so much trouble to get them?" Palla scolded me. The baby slurped. I guessed he was getting something.

"I was the one went to the trouble," Gawene told her sister, "and look, the boy's come, and ruined his shoes to boot." I liked to think Wene was always defending me.

"I'm sure Arn's waiting out in the car, huh Chab? Why don't you run ask your daddy in for cake?"

"Look at the fella's feet, girl. Arn made him walk."

"All the way from the Illinois apartments? Arn's not a cruel man." It's true, Dad never hit me. I was more likely to bop him for being so bone-addled.

"If Arn sent you out in this weather," Tim said, "he must mean you to take the merchandise home in plastic, and that I don't have."

I hated to say I had not come for Dad. Though I expected Dad's knock any second, if he'd escaped The Face. Rain should scare a crackerjack, but one short of cash for his next pebbles could walk through waterfalls. Dad might bumble codes but still guess my mind.

Gawene came and helped me sit up. Her eyes wore highbeams so bright I wondered why the lights were on. She had those up-flying pencil eyebrows you see on older white women in agencies, but Wene couldn't be twenty. Those eyebrows pulled her whole wide face skyward. I fished out of my pockets the wads I'd nipped from Dad. The loot flicked drops. You never hold out the greens before the metal is in hand, but cash was the only voice I had at the moment. Gawene's beams got even brighter.

With some grunts, Tim Stevens stood. "Hold your claws, Wene, I'll track his order." Dad had always called Tim Stevens the only honest cluck out there.

Modest Dad, never put himself on the list of honest clucks. I wasn't making any honesty list soon. Given that wheels are faster than shoes, I was surprised I was still here on my mission, whatever that was.

Tim Stevens brought a flat open carton, in it the five sawed-offs. His whitened hands gripped the box just fine. Crackerjacks are always maiming themselves.

I was standing by the door already. My feet had turned into beds of hot rocks. "You think if you rush fast enough," Tim said, "you can dodge the raindrops?"

"If Arn don't have the decency to drive over in this weather," Palla said, "don't go piling those guns on that boy."

"He's old enough to stand up to that little man," Gawene said. She shifted a strap that had wandered down a bare arm. Bare arms in February.

"Chab, did your daddy ever lay a hand on you?" Palla said. She pulled the baby from her shirt, and he released his mouth with a smack. Gawene took him and stood him on her thighs and toggled his nose and grinned and hummed, like she was showing how I could treat a certain little man. Her thick hair tips just touched her bare shoulders.

"You remember your Mom bouncing you?" Gawene said. I didn't answer, and she said, "You know I had a hunch who she was."

"You don't know anyone's business," Palla scolded her.

"He had to have a mom once."

"You don't know anyone's business."

Everyone hushed up. I kept holding out the green stuff. Tim glanced at it but handed me the carton without taking the wad. I had to take that carton of metal in both arms to keep from teetering off my flaming hind paws. Now the box covered the payup hand. Tim was scowling, had to see through my sham, down to my robbery of Dad. I just let the money dribble to the floor and freed the hand for a better grip. My swag on the carpet looked to be about one-fifty, in tens and twenties, not too low an amount in my expert judgment, considering the boodle was wholesale. No one had talked prices. Tim bowed over, scowling.

My foot scuffed the door open, and I shouldered through the screen. Past the porch, the rain taps came fast on box and metal.

5.

I felt eyes at the door watching my wet neck fade beyond the streetlight. As long as I felt them, a warm place seemed to be waiting for me ahead. Then turning off Moore onto Morrell stole me from their view, and Morrell dropped into the Corinth Street valley. Down there you find only abandoned Jack-in-the-Boxes and tumbling brake shops and hardly any headlights on big old Corinth. I stopped under the blinking yellow light. At least, back at the golf course, when I'd seen I'd broken with Dad, Tim Stevens's had been ahead. In my carton, water trickled.

South on Corinth was that complex of apartment units which is the twin of ours back on Illinois. Except these were algae green, not puddle tan. Now why you would have these two brother clumps of ugly buildings miles apart, only the city and the nineteen-fifties could tell. Dad had made a few trades here. While he would be off scrounging a dime of hamburger helper, he'd let the cub play in the hollowed-out units.

I knew at least two basements, with only small animals to scare away. From Corinth, a lane and two lines of trees wind up the hill. A vision of coconut grove paradise must have drugged those fifties builders. I only saw large dark skeletons, called post oaks. The basement I aimed for was on the second row up, third unit on the right. In front stood a platoon of old water heaters, probably pried out by a cluck bent on selling the copper pipes. Why he placed them all at one unit, ask his boubou mind. But that basement still had a deadbolt on its door you could lock from inside. I opened and hollered, "Ho there, Hettie," whoever Hettie was. Only answer, some very small feet.

It reeked of carpet soggy too long, rodent piss stagnant too long. My box was about to collapse my legs, but I gripped it under arm to deadbolt the door. Then I listened. Drips came from everywhere, and only half of that outside.

In the dark my feet knew their way down the steps, like ours at home but without the steel hatch door. A banister started the same place, halfway down, once you passed the ceiling. Underfoot, though, the carpet here squished. At the bottom, to the right, was a wall, and a door into the only room. Back home, Dad had ripped out this wall years ago so he could always watch the stairs, as if his steel hatch did not guard enough.

Through the door I saw a light, if you could call it that, a square of charcoal gray just a shade lighter than black, the high window. In these units the basement windows are below ground level and look onto a square concrete well about two feet deep, an air shaft. That's the window Dad had bricked up. This one, I just made out, had bars.

But not enough gray sifted through to show me my feet. I kicked through a stretch of emptiness, near tripping because I kept expecting to hit something harder than trash. Already the shivers took over. The chill whistled through the bars. Somebody squeaked, warning its young. My toes struck something soft and firm, and I bent and felt: a mattress. It came just in time for my collapse. The goods clanked out of their box.

City Limit

The mattress was moist. I pulled off the moist Forzieris, careful not to tear the valuable skin and leather. The ice got cozy with the sores. At the same time I was shaking from the butt upwards. Wet clothes, wet body, damp floor, dank bed, and the skeleton trees were rattling. If you take all your duds off, you're still soaked.

And those broken guns? How could I find parts to sell them and buy a sandwich? I just might have a second tiny wad of Dad's still down my water glued pocket, if it hadn't spilled onto Tim Stevens's floor. But how was I going to walk anywhere in these feet? I was no cluck and had no endless connections to other clucks and their paranoias to sell to. All Dad's clucks I knew already had their protection. I had cut out on Dad because he kept mangling his codes to the point I feared The Face's rampage? But Dad had his Coleman stove, he was dry! If I was so smart, why was I cold?

I crawled about the room, hands and knees, keeping my busted heels safe and high. But I found nothing more and returned to home mattress. I put on my socks, hoping my feet would find some temperature, and crawled up under a dank mattress.

6.

You don't sleep underwater. I got wetter by the minute till I threw off the mattress and paced in a three foot square to avoid smashing my small housemates. But the bare feet only drank up the chill, so I scooted back under the mattress and peeled off my soppy nylon jacket. In a few hours I warmed up a patch of mattress water above and of carpet water below.

When I looked out on a gray room, the brown skeletons outside were still dripping. I watched the swirls in the plaster ceiling and took some seconds to recall last night and the fact that the ceiling was not Dad's. The carpet was blue not orange, or had been blue before mildew speckled it black. There was a rectangle in the wall's paint where the fridge had been, and a stove beside it. A round electric burner dangled by a wire. That kitchenette was right where Dad's was, the wall opposite the stairs. Under the barred window there were three large cartons. So someone had staked out the basement, maybe still frequented it. I would never touch those boxes. Wadded sacks and opened yogurt and milk containers spilled across the floor. Birds gave off that happy morning sound that I never really trusted.

I lay and lay. You know those gray mornings when the throat is scratchy as toast and the upper sinus is sparking. My carpet of a bed and mattress of a cover were comfortable now. At least, when I reached and felt, my socks were slightly drier than liquid. I refitted my Forzieris over them. Last night's spikes had dulled to good round pain.

With a lot of hiccups, the kitchen faucet finally spat brown fluid. A minute of flow cleared much of the color, and since it didn't smell I cupped hands and drank. It was almost as good as food.

Next came a meeting with my swag. The open carton lay alongside the mattress, collapsing from its soak. All double-barreled, four were Remington .410-gauge and one a Winchester 16. Droplets beaded the varnished wood stocks and the short double-barrels and breaches. The barrels had been hacked off so crudely the brighter metal of the cut shone in a ring. Whoever the slop-jobber was had not lathed the edges smooth.

The breaches on a couple of them needed some force to shut. Others were so loose the barrel almost flew off the hinge when you opened. The pins wanted attention or replacement. Attention demanded tools. And tools you had to acquire, either free or paid for. I practically hugged the gun in best shape, the Winchester, wishing I could take the quickest route and munch it directly.

Now, where to stash my future while I was out shopping, since the door had no lock? I imagined, if The Face had spared him, then Dad was combing the city and would catch me with the merchandise. Really I had no clue what he would do when he found the wampum missing. He would probably discover it faster than his missing tool boy. I had left him some cash for the week. The worst crime I'd ever done before, and that pretty regularly, was sneaking change now and then for vanilla crèmes I'd buy after school and promptly dispatch. But he counted only bills, in fact fives and up. Boubou makes you think big, lose the details.

How big a detail was I?

Across Corinth were some woods going up the slope, exposed though, with their dresses off for winter. I used to poke in them when Dad dealt in this complex, and I knew a stack of rotten pallets not too useful for hobo clucks. Just the thought of those pallets for safekeeping, I had a business plan. Sell some guns, buy some food, then more guns.

I pulled on my liquid jacket, like sliding into a mud hole, and lugged my haul up the steps.

7.

The pallets were hacked and splintered across the leaf litter. Some gick monster must have chased his visions of glory with a pickax. The bare trees on this steep hillside left me exposed. My box of contraband was in plain sight of the traffic drowsing along Corinth below me.

On top the hill a line of backyard fences leaned like they were holding back the woods. Behind one fence a Doberman with clipped ears and tail shook its tags at me. Just my side of the fence was the kind of pit folks dig off their property to dispose of chairs and fridges. Branches covered it. I made out a plastic doghouse under them, probably this animal's old hangout. Few clucks would choose to sleep ten feet from his nose.

I climbed on. The Forzieris slid about and reported old wounds. Discarded cement chunks under the leaf rot surprised my feet. The dog stood against the leaning chain link fence, so the fence leaned more. After the climb I had to catch breath, trying not to look at him. The doghouse door faced him, good for my boodle's safety but not for mine. He belly danced. His uplifted nose neared the fence's top bar. Finally I held my breath and strode to the hut like it was mine. He said nothing until I bent through the door and my arms rubbed it. He let out the screeches that dogs save for fire trucks. The hind paws scuffed. I dropped the box inside and scrambled just as a curtain flicked in master's home.

After slipsliding down the hill, my socked little toe was peeking out the seam I'd opened last night. My heart rattled away, more than from the exercise. The dog rattled away, too. And all the way down through the trees came the sound of paws thumping the fence posts.

8.

Dad was right. I inhaled too many fried pork skins, and now I was winded. And I need food even more than gun parts.

As I slogged up Corinth, I felt my ass waddle, like I'd seen in plenty large families paddling down the sidewalks. At least you knew they didn't chow down hamburger helper. The Monday traffic on Corinth was skimpier than the Sunday. There's nowhere to go to work to around here. Corinth is a wide boulevard with an island of lamp posts curving through the wooded valley, and you see how somebody back in the fifties saw a pretty future. The rain was picking up again, so I pulled out the tiny bump in my pocket before water got it stuck again. Bless the government's cotton fibers that keep print intact, I unwadded—a five and two ones. And held them tight.

Up Corinth past Morrell you have a yellow burger shack, little more than a cube of plywood and a hand-scrawled sign. On the outside glass, I saw me approaching, my hair like the fluff you sweep off the linoleum. The black Coogis could pass for a couple duffle bags, the matted jacket for a shower curtain. In these wrinkles, I looked even wider. Now here's a presentation package, Dad. What am I selling, counterfeit State Fair tickets?

The Burger Mecca interior has about enough standing room for three me's, and I was the only this morning. I stared out the window, searching for my own customers, and that burger, bite by bite, made the rain slow down. The girl said, "Your eyes are asking for seconds." At ninety-nine cents, you could go without lettuce and bacon. My second one killed the rain before I finished. The sun was pushing through the clouds.

The whole morning, I walked down Corinth, back up High Hat Blvd., as Dad miscalled it, over as far as Bonnie View and back down Morrell. I calculated I ought to sell the one piece that looked in working order, the Winchester, then buy parts for the others and keep what pennies I could for food. Last night's feet were telling me why nobody, at least of the sort who might need my wares, was strolling in this weather. Only folks in dungarees and other workclothes were sloshing out to their cars. Women along the dirt roadside were balancing umbrellas over tots. Any second now, Dad's '78 Honda would pull over and bundle his own tot out of the rain.

That window curtain at the Doberman master's home kept flicking in my mind, until it brought back the drizzle.

It must have been afternoon, as far as I could tell through the gray, when the beamers started showing up on their porches. They kept the same hours as those back home on Illinois. There's a lower population density of them here in these small, kind homes. Dad says the palaces in the city's far north can be boneheaded too. Here, they come outside rubbing the pain of light from their eyes with their fingertips. They move in jerks. Their shins poke out their car doors while they henpeck the floor for crumbs. Maybe anyone else passing by would just see folks at home. Dad taught me how to see.

On Bonnie View is the long flat junior high with its fields, and facing it a row of tiny wood homes. A gentleman in a brown suit, no shirt, stood at his wooden fence, watching the schoolyard and doing the jitter dance, foot to foot. The no shirt in the freezing rain cued me too. The time was pushing on five o'clock, school long out, a few kids screaming in the fields. The gentleman was a couple houses away, but I got winded just pushing my shoes along. That is, I was not ready for a first sales effort.

Hands in pants pockets, he sneered. I felt he had all the protection he needed, in those pockets, and was about to protect himself from a stranger.

Before he jerked again, I said, "Need a piece?"

"I don't need your piper ass, asshole."

"I mean a gat."

"I ain't taking no hot gat off a no narc."

"I'm not a narc. I got a fine 16 sawed-off. I'll go get it."

"Now get, afore I saw off that rentboy ass."

His hand jerked in his pocket, and I scatted on. Once he was behind me, my back crawled up and down my shirt, waiting for a blast. I was never selling those guns and I hoped that dog's master had taken them from the doghouse, and I had to go back to Dad crying like I had not in four years since he made me quit school.

My ass shimmied along Areba Street. I don't know why, must have been a need to prove my success as a salesman, but I made another pitch. A woman wearing so much red she looked the fruit raspberry lounged in an old Trans Am front passenger seat, window open to the drizzle. I spoke as I passed. She shoved her head out. "Shove your gun down that deep throat and pull the trigger, fudge packer." She shrieked so, I fingered my ears.

After Areba, Hutchins Street runs above the slope of the apartment units that twin my old home grounds. I dropped down High Hat Blvd. and its two sweet winding columns of brown skeletons. At the second row from the bottom, third unit over, there was the basement I'd made my runaway's camp, ages ago already. The army of water heaters still guarded the front. In the dusk that comes on early under ugly clouds, I just made out that the basement window was lit.

Then the light flickered, like a sputter from a Coleman lantern element. Who fussed with white-gas lanterns but Dad? Everyone else liked the convenience and safety of battery-powered. Dad could have found out I'd stopped by Tim Stevens's, then guessed I'd ditched myself in one of these units where I used to play. He was waiting me out on my own new turf. Now I had only the doghouse.

The rain, of course, picked up, in angry balls.

At the bottom of the hill I crossed Corinth into the woods and reason hit me. Dad's only sense of mission was his next crumb of boubou. He could plan one step ahead, that is sell guns and at the same time buy boubou. He would be unable to insert one extra step, that is wait here for the boy who makes the gun sales possible. The boubou killed long term planning ability. That light could not be Dad's.

Then insight of a lifetime hit me: Dad always mixed boubou purchase with gun sale. You had to, to ease your way into the customer's trust.

I recrossed Corinth and climbed back up High Hat, spying up and down the rows of units. There were groups of two or three folks, big groups of five or ten, at a car fender or around an upended barrel for monte. If only the sun came back, I'd have my pick of clientele, loners or pairs with the bored lookout for sale. Down my row of units, my basement window still glowed, and I pushed my knees along just in case Dad was peeking from that window.

There must be three dozen units along High Hat, and it's steep and the wind was bleeding out of me again. I stopped, panting like those phony wrestlers you see on TV who look around for someone to harass. It's said that fat can keep you alive for weeks; my stomach never heard such a thing. But burger funds had to go into seeding a big sale. I turned and spotted my man.

Almost nightfall and he was wearing shades, a good sign of a cluck. He strutted about a patch of dirt formerly a yard, with a cell phone as if really talking to anyone. They're always just wrapping up business when you walk in.

"Sell dimes?" I said.

"Hold on, hold on, Phil, I'll get back wicha," he said. He snapped the phone shut. "I don't do dimes. Only bones and boulders."

The usual start. Whenever you ask to buy, no one asks if you're a narc. This guy couldn't be eighteen, skinny face smooth as my own baby mug. I didn't have enough for a dime, only five bucks, and they hate nickels. But when I got him down to a nickel he whined, I mean like a five-year-old. "I ain't dicing up no pee-wees. You said a dime."

But you just pull out cash, and this guy was so green even five bucks grew the golfball eyes. He spat many times around himself and almost on me, but in minutes he tugged the plastic sack out of the coat pocket and dipped right in for a glassine nickel ready-made, of course. He cursed and complained and spat, even when he pocketed the five. And I let out as casual as possible, like an afterthought—it helped he was such a kid—"Want a piece? Sawed-off. Winchester 16."

The golfballs came back. He was looking at my presentation shoes. "Sawed-off? What you punk doing with a sawed-off? How much?"

I got too happy feeling a sale was heating and did opposite what you should. I blurted way on the low side, "Thirty." That was about what I'd paid Tim Stevens for it.

His eyes jittered around the grounds like he was seeking adult guidance. "Thirty for a sawed-off. That a toy?" His gold chain laughed at me. I should have gone triple what I said. Thank my shoes. Dad often went one-twenty, one-fifty for a piece I'd oiled and shined. But I'd barely glanced this Winchester in daylight, and it could be a dog owner's delight by now.

"I'll go forty if thirty's too low," I said, and you never start going up.

"Forty! You said thirty. You can't back down. Now how'm I going to see this piece? You ain't got it in your pocket. All I see is strawberry milkshakes."

But he was holding his breath. My upping tactic was pumping value into my deal. I had way more years than him and a lot less boubou in the brain. "You wait here ten minutes?"

He nodded and thrust hands in pants pockets like he was pushing his limbs into the dirt. I took off uphill to Hutchins, to go back the long way around, down Morrell to Corinth. So I avoided showing the customer the direction of the warehouse.

When I kicked through the damp leaves below the doghouse, the sky had that metallic blue that a gray day hits for two minutes before it drops to charcoal. The dog stood on its hind paws, leaning into the fence as if it had been waiting since I'd left. His eyes caught the sky glow and turned it yellow. But this time the dog said nothing, and I crunched twigs every step to the doghouse. Then I saw what kept him quiet. In a tree shadow not ten feet off stood a human shadow.

The shadow spoke. "That your prize stash of metal in my doggie house?"

9.

He froze me about one foot away from seeing into the doghouse. I had no clue if the prize stash remained. I only had the feeling that if he was standing out in this icy rain waiting for me, he must be badly offended I would use his doggie house.

I said, "Sorry."

The dog released its front paw hold on the fence and settled onto all fours.

The man said, "Jeffrey still likes to sleep out there on rowdy nights, and I didn't want any guns to scare him."

Near the dog I noticed a fence gate with one of those two-prong latches you can padlock. This one was missing the padlock. You could push up the latch with your nose. Darkness was about to finish us off.

I said, "I'm really sorry, I didn't know this was a rowdy night."

"Tonight's not. He'll be sleeping on the porch after I dry him off. But don't be sorry. I like that Winchester, and if you're stashing, you must be selling. I'd like to buy."

His offer shocked me so much I giggled. He was poking fun of me, and I was going along. Why would he keep a doghouse on city land? He had to have stolen all five in my collection.

The customer stepped out of the tree shadow. He wore a brimmed hat shiny from shellac coating or rain. The sky had already gone charcoal, but city light bounces off that kind of sky. He said, "I mean it. You own them guns, or you just the runner?"

"Own."

"What're you asking for the Winchester?"

I was biting that inner part of your lip that feels like pellets inside wet plastic. An hour ago I was in poverty, now I had two bidders for the same merchandise. I blurted, shouted even, "Sixty."

"Sixty!" The dog barked too. "You sure you're the owner?"

"Fifty!"

"God, dang, just give it away, then. I thought that thing looked in working order."

Here I was going the wrong direction for price again: down this time. But my head was twirling. "I'll throw in a nickel bag."

"Take your god be-damned cocaine and keep it off my property. I just want the gun. You said fifty, and I said I'll take it, and that's a deal under the code of law."

I dug into that dark soggy doghouse and felt for the Winchester by the swirly insignia at the breach. If he had waited around for the rightful owner, then maybe I could trust him with my inventory for twenty-four more hours.

At the gate he flicked open the latch with one finger. The dog stayed at master's side, wagging and whining like it wanted a biscuit. The transaction passed through the open gate. I received a small stack of what must have mostly been ones. I wasn't going to provoke a customer by checking his addition.

I said, "If tonight's not too rowdy and Jeffrey's sleeping out, could I keep the rest of the stash in his house? They're all broken anyway."

His turn to chuckle. I'd provoked more joy out of one trade than Dad had in six years' worth. Up close, my customer was big as a casket, face round and light under that hat, long mustache. He might have been Mexican though he didn't sound it, or white. "You jail bait? You don't seem fifteen."

People always guess me older than I am. Size pays. "Eighteen soon. I'm a high tenor in choir."

"I don't need a liar in my doghouse."

"The sale's legal because it's private and you can buy from any age and I ain't a felon."

"Do what you have to tonight. Just don't do your shady business up here."

He shut the latch, still no padlock. The dog stayed, nose at the latch.

I groped through my wares for the Remington in the best shape for the kid below. The remark about liar stung. I had been in choir once at William Brown Miller. And I'd be eighteen soon enough, if I made it past this evening.

One Remington's breach wasn't too loose when opened, and it actually locked. When I slid down the slick leaves, under the branches it was totally dark. Up High Hat the kid was at an orange streetlight. I waved him to a shadow and took out the purchase. He didn't even run a finger along the grip but grabbed the piece and slapped paper in my hand. I counted at once, a ten and twenty, and he scatted.

Long day. A thick warm glow in my pocket. Burger Mecca ahead.

10.

The light in my old apartment, last night's apartment that is, shined away. No head peeked out. The dark protected me enough to stop and study the window awhile. When I came to the army of water heaters, the light moved off the window glass and flew away. It had been the reflection of another unit's door light.

Dad, my holy ghost.

Still, who knows he wasn't in that apartment. I crawled up dog hill. The doghouse was drier than the basement but rockier. There was still the dripping, this time from a few thousand trees. Sometimes they rained on the plastic roof in gusts. And the smell was dog and earth instead of rat-pee carpet, and outside somebody's collar tags kept tinkling. The plan that shut my eyes went like this: Next day, I was fixing and selling the broken three and coming home with a profit for Dad.

I'm telling you it's been six-and-a-half, seven years since that night I walked out, Suds.

In that bumpy doghouse, I was dreaming how I could be sitting by the Coleman lantern with my magazines. Was he ranting about Jehovah and Buddha, if I wasn't there to ignore him? Dad always brought home from the trash all kinds of magazines, on yachting, hunting, travel, bottle collecting, mothering, lots in Spanish I don't know, even tittie magazines, he didn't look, just plopped the stack on the floor for me. I found out some weird things. Do you know, every year in Cuba they make 100,000 tons of worm humus? That's earthworm shit, and people spread it on farms to help sugar and rice grow. I was glad potatoes did not make the list, since I like fries. But a ton, I'd calculated as I read the article, 2000 pounds, that was about 11 of me by last measure. Then 100,000 of that, how could puny earthworms eat so much? I'd have to find Cuba someday and see this. It's far outside Dallas.

They did say the worms could be dried and ground up into powder, for use in places like—burgers. Well, I don't know if worms are worse than cows in that regard.

I slept anyway. I had sure better sleep, with three burgers, two fries and one tin of Altoids under belt. I use mints as a form of tooth-brushing.

And I must have power slept. Next day, I woke not to my big plans but to what sounded like 100,000 loads of buckshot hitting the ground. I looked out the doghouse door: It was rain, 2000 times harder than yesterday. A flash flood like I used to see in the creek behind William Brown Miller was my present bed. My down jacket was so soaked it was flat. Even the big tough dog got to sit it out indoors. And I was sneezing, throat jagged as a hacksaw, a full blasted cold.

The merchandise was swimming. The carton was a limp strip of lasagna.

It took till noon to let the rain calm down and to gather enough joy to go hit the day. First I did a full checkup on the remaining goods, which wanted surgery. I would need a few gunsmithing basics that I could have gotten for free from a certain Illinois Avenue apartment: a firing pin tool, standard allen wrench set, hinge pins and reamer, nylon/brass punch with punch tips to remove some trigger plate pins, mainspring tool to change the mainsprings, torque wrench for fingerguard screws. And a magnetic law enforcement screwdriver handle wouldn't hurt.

On the trudge to Harran's Gun and Supply way up off East Jefferson, the blisters about bubbled out of the Forzieris. I thought of adding a bonesaw to my list, to remove a couple of feet. Harran's front glass door showed me myself again, and I'd taken another tumbling since yesterday. I bowed my head to miss the sight. Harran behind the counter must have caught my act. "If it isn't Chabney Gullo, hiding his face."

Harran's was no place to walk in proud. The front window hid the store's insides behind posterboard with pistols falling off their wires. Their barrels were brown with dust. Inside smelled less fresh than my basement of two nights ago. Humidity beaded on the wood trimming, wood ceilings and walls, wood counters. The wood floor felt squishy under your toes. Cheap old secondhand .22 rifles and deer guns nobody wanted sagged on the walls. Since he had to register gun buyers, he lost plenty business to the likes of Dad and me. But he was happy to serve us with parts and tools, because at least he sold something. Then our customers came for the boxes of shells that lined two walls behind glass.

"Your daddy was hunting for ya yesterday," he said.

I have to admit, I think I swayed like an iron had tapped my head. Dad had escaped The Face. And he was actually asking about me.

Yet I got a wind of glad for missing him here at Harran's. I said, "Yeah, we kinda passed each other somewhere."

"He came in twice."

Now I was nervous. Stupidly I looked behind out the door. "It was a long day all right."

"I thought maybe you were hanging your head on account of you two being lost."

"We got caught in bad storms. And we need some of our tools again."

"I can see the cold coming down you." He handed me a tissue from the box of wipes for cleaning loupes. He had his old-fashioned ways. "Time you're out of the rain."

Dad was alive as ever. Too bad I had this cold. Harran might think I was crying.

I spouted the list, and he wrote on a pad with his chin thrust out. He's thin and tries to fill up the lost space by wearing a down vest like a real huntsman, even when the shop melts in June. His big head gives a look of bigness, with the classic gray beard and bald spot of regular gun folks. But he always squints and slides his lips over each other with a slippery sound like a silly old schoolteacher. This visit was my first alone. He swiped the sheet off the pad, no further questions, and went poking through the back shelves. He's a good businessman. Dad says he was one of the last whites from when Oak Cliff was white in the fifties, before the blacks and the rest of us moved in.

He totaled up the goods with a pencil. His cash register was the wooden type that pokes up the numbers in a glass display on top and tings. But the numbers were permanently at 21.57. My total almost wiped out last night's success, 72.78. Harran tries to give you as much used and discount as he can, so you won't go to Ray's Sporting Goods over on Singleton. But some items, like the magnetic law enforcement screwdriver handle that I just had to have, you only find full retail.

City Limit

He counted my stack of ones and squinted at me behind the thrust-out chin. He must do the chin bit to gain height. Dad never carried so many oners.

"We'll be back, I bet," I said. Harran said nothing; he had to know what was happening. But he was too knowledgeable a businessman to interfere.

Sun was actually coming out while I tightened a trigger hold in the dog house. My magnetic law enforcement screwdriver handle, I mean with the screwdriver tip, did the trick for one damn loose breach hinge. Dog was out again, watching my work. His breath vapor looked thick in the sunlight. Tonight would freeze my jacket. I felt I was inserting screws against time.

Around dinner time, the dog's master came out, with a loud slam of the back door on its spring. He dumped the dog its gallon of nibbles from the sack, then started my way, with his look anywhere but me like he had no intention of visiting me. And he came out the gate and visited me. He invited me to dinner.

His wife had been gone a couple years (left him, he meant). I don't know why folks like Tim Stevens you do gun business with feel they have to share bread too. I guess it's to make up for the life that the purchase is bound to take away. Who wants to risk eating with a big friendly gun-toting divorcee? I said I'd just stuffed myself with burgers.

I went and stuffed myself at Burger Mecca and two days later sold all three guns.

11.

But first I had to lug the three of them and a bellyful of burger down from the doghouse and up High Hat. My old quarters had a taker, not Dad as I found out when I opened the door and hollered "Hettie, you there?" I dropped into another basement I knew a few units away, same familiar reek of mold but not the rodent piss. This place lacked the mattress I didn't miss but a stove remained, electric, one burner dangling off the side by a wire. The fusebox was in the same place as back home, in the bathroom wall. Switching the fuses, I found one that worked, so the burner coil heated up. Sometimes even the electric company is not a responsible parent and lets you freeload.

My coat dried that night on a big tree branch I set up like a wino's hotdog toaster. But I was flipflopping all night on a floor much smoother than last night's and warmer if you can use the term. Sometimes it's bad to have had enough sleep, then you're too rested to sleep frozen. Next day my cold was flowing, but not a drop from the tap to wash up. Up the same hill as the dog, in a dumping ground, I dug up a blanket and lamp and unscrewed a door lock. I found a cheap bulb at the discounters up Corinth. I put the lock on my upstairs door and patched the lamp to an empty stove wire. Locked in and lit up, what more for a home? Home enough till I could work my way back to the real one. I only had to watch for sparks from that wire patch job until I could afford electrical tape.

Turning the three pieces into master pieces took the rest of the afternoon under the lamp. All three breaches snapped into place clean as ice when you shut them, the triggers clicked under the finger, the firing pins pounded the bone of my pinky. I celebrated by killing my cash at the Mecca.

And I demolished my Forzieris next day making gun sales.

The sky lay off harassing me and my soles. I strayed as far as Marsalis and its zoo parking lot. But visitors in their big groups floating back to the parking lot did not look the types seeking protection from humans. Then on my way back east to Cedar Crest and the alphabet avenues near the Trinity River, I caught a fish. Old man, at least older than Dad, got to talking to me outside his shanty. I reminded him of his son, "stocky" he put it. He was too beefy himself to be a gick monster. An out of work car mechanic, long ago he'd moved from the countryside into town where it was "actually safer." And then the kids went traveling, and sadly his instinct was proved right. He'd lost one son to a misfortune in the countryside. I suggested a vigilante machine for his jacket. He said why not. The two miles to the stash and back sank another toe hole in my leather.

The next sale took until nightfall, a woman who accosted me. She had seen me pass hours ago with what appeared a gunstock poking under my jacket. I had an inkling her request would find use in her marriage. I was fetching the item, when three kids jumped me. They were pulling a scarf around my neck for a good squeeze. Before the blood left my head, I got the Remington from the jacket. They fell back and stared with puffball eyes. "Please don't!" They were age eight to twelve. The ten lost his puffballs first. "I sure like that better than a scarf. Where can I get one?" The day was teaching me to let the customer come to me. They employed their pockets, and I hobbled back to the hill and my last prize, for the lady. That night, under my lamp, I counted 188.56.

Now, should I go on to Dad's right away, tonight?

Those kids only had to scrounge up some change to land them some shells.

All five toes of both feet stared at me through their socks and the toes of the shoes. They wore red puffballs themselves. The presentation package was finished.

12.

Something stronger than hunger made my decision about what adventures to go on tonight. It came down as a black iron balloon in my head. Exhaustion. I woke to gray bird-chatter.

I sat up with a pang. I'd left Dad alone another night. And I had enough money to pay him back and even pocket some for vanilla crèmes. It seemed cruel to have left him just because he confused his codes, when he'd bought my shoes for years.

Before I went anywhere, the footgear needed attention. How would he feel if I showed up with bloated feet? I peeled off the socks, and they stuck to the skin, rather to the open sores. In the open air, the white and red craters and volcanoes burned, as if I'd sprayed salt on them. I rotated the socks, once lime now chocolate, because the toes of different feet make different holes. I tore a shirt I'd found two days ago, near the lock and lamp I'd scrounged from the hillside, and wrapped the shoes. They flapped like alligator mouths, my feet being the tongues. I clamped the mouths shut, and they looked sad-eyed in their blue bandages. Maybe yesterday's kid customers would not be tempted to hold me up. I pulled on a man's red velveteen shirt I'd dried on the stick. It had an oil track across it, but after all the rain and sun it was less beaten than mine.

Going up the stairs, I kneeled and crawled. Outside and down the hill, I stopped every few trees, leaned and held up one foot, then the other, though the pain didn't stop.

Some hours later at the discount center, I bought socks and tried on cloth sneakers, imitation Keds. They should not give my two bloated winos bedsores like hard leather would. Luckily you take your own measurements there and track down the shoebox yourself, because I was smelling myself as I knotted laces. The checkout clerk worked his nose anyway, but maybe it was at my lowly selection. Clerks at discount centers can be snootier than their upscale pals, because they have so much further to go. He spotted my bare feet, without wrinkling the nose.

The woolly socks and kind shoes still felt like bulldozers on my blisters as I crossed Thornton Expressway on Eighth. Then where Eighth jogs in front the graveyard, it struck me: All these public roads I'm traipsing, Dad should have found me. If he was searching, he would have asked a couple customers, say on High Hat, and someone would have seen me.

And I saw it: At Harran's, he hadn't been asking for me. He'd been buying supplies and gabbing when he'd let slip I was gone.

He wasn't looking. He didn't give me a thought. How would he stay alive?

I needed a bath. And so did my pants. Someone nearby had to have enough family to keep an operating tub. There were the Blokurgs on Monaghan, who always had a steady stream of Lugers from overseas, wherever that was. But they were too familylike and might call the truant officers. Katie Storey on Bobbie kept her skin and hair shiny, but she was a raspberry, bought Dad's kokomo with methods other than cash while I sat in the car. And raspberries ask payment just for the time off their watch. Husker Metcalf lived around the corner from her on Viaduct, above the riverbottoms. He machined crankshafts in his back hut, from specs for all models of cars, his legitimate business. Nobody bought them, so they cluttered his dirt yard, even his bathroom. He also machined his own designs of pistols, which people did buy, wacky stuff like revolvers with giant twelve-shell cylinders. He wouldn't mind if I washed up, but I'd come out of his tub greasier than I went in.

And there were the Stevenses, just off Morrell. Their clothes looked ironed twice daily. It had been days since my rainy visit, but with a second drop-in in a row from me all alone, their worry about family might shift into overdrive. They did have Dad's cell number. So I could test Dad, see if he really needed his fixer back. Anyway, even on this blowy cold day, I smelled myself.

Soon I was standing on that long covered porch, waiting for an answer. The rain on the beige wood planks had dried, leaving smudges from the overflowing drainpipes. Last time here in the icy rain I lay on my belly to avoid the foot nuisance. This time in the dry sun I simply shifted foot to foot and winced. Noon, and gick monsters are still sleeping off last night's orgy.

Half a day later the window curtain flicked with someone's cry of shock, and Gawene opened the door. She grew some puffballs. "Chabney? Haven't you combed your hair since last time?"

She reached out and whopped down a growth from the crown of my head. I felt it bob right back out of place. My black hair looks straight but can be as stubborn as comb teeth. Once rain and bad sleep get a hold of it, it can point surprising directions.

"Tim and Palla are out," she went on. She was looking around me toward the street. "I'n't your dad waiting for you?"

I blew through my lips, tired of my nutty lack of answers. She had done her hair, cut at the neck, curls going inward, in that stiff way only black women's straightened hair can do. And she'd dyed it a purple red. That's with deep blue lipstick, blush on the wide cheeks, blue eyeliner. She looked too pretty for a real girl, pretty in that way of a boy trying hard to look a girl.

"I swear, Chabney, your pants are awful. And that shirt has axle grease. Your daddy used to take such good care, I was so proud of you two."

"Are you busy? If nobody's there, could I use your shower?"

I shut my eyes after I said it, because I didn't mean to give myself away so fast. When I opened them she was gawking again. "Y'all's shower broke?"

"I'm not sure."

She let me in but kept the stare. It seemed she was looking over a purchase she should not have made. Boubou can give that effect to the eyes, but I had seen her cranking before, like that rainy night, without this once-over.

"I promise I don't want to interrupt," I said.

She was leading me slowly to the bathroom with glances backward. The place still reeked of burnt sugar and acetone. The living room walls were bare, but the hallway, first time I'd seen it, had a few dozen photos in frames. Black and white and color, must have been family, many on big empty fields, farms I guessed, not golf courses, which don't have large animals.

"This is about the weirdest request I've had," she said. "Bath in the middle of the day from a kid like you showing up on my porch."

I'd heard about the sorts of requests raspberries get, but I wasn't giving her no lip because I didn't know if she was a raspberry and I hated to hurt Gawene's feelings. Not all girl gick monsters are skeegers. I said, "Dad come by?"

She halted and turned in the bathroom door like she'd changed her mind. "Chabney, you gonna tell me what's going on." See, when I speak up I give myself away.

The bathroom was pink tile with a bare bulb high up a painted plaster ceiling. Cutesie pictures cluttered all four walls, drawings of baby-type humans with giant heads and teensy bodies and eyes taking half the face and their pants fallen down their feet and saying stuff like "Whoopsie-daisy!"

"Was I right?" she said. "That night you were here, your daddy made you walk all the way in the rain?"

If she could stare at me, I could stare at her pictures. One had a giant-headed girl and boy. The girl's stick body had some laundry bag breasts. The boy was squeezing one, and out came liquid. Somebody was saying, "Peek-a-Boo!" I noticed all the baby-headed humans were white, with big pink circles for cheeks, and I felt bad for her. Maybe they had come with the house, or were all her sister Palla's.

"I see you got some new shoes," she said and threw a towel at me like my shoes upset her, then left the room. I looked down at them, for any stray pricetags. How could she have told they were new?

Taking off my pants, I hated touching them, first time off since that day I left Dad. They crackled in my fingers. I tried looking at the ceiling as if that way I could avoid the odor. I put the money and other pocket stuff on the sink top behind the sack of diapers and turned the hot tap on the clothes. Once they were underwater and I could stand looking, I dumped in shampoo. The water was already sort of a cherry coke.

The bathtub squatted on four claws. and the curtain went all the way around it. Of course that water felt like rainbows for the skin. After some minutes, Gawene opened the door and came in. The curtain was fuzzy clear, so I could see her shape and shirt color and she had to see my shape and skin color. She poked through a cabinet. She couldn't see the money out because of baby bottles in the way. I turned away, looking over my shoulder. She was poking an awful long time. It wasn't right she would barge in on a guest like this, and I wished she'd find her item, but then, she was making me comfortable at-home. But she found her thing, went out and shut the door.

After rinsing my hair, I was just in the dreamy stage of how long should I stay under, when the door opened again. This time I couldn't see her shirt color. Instead there was a white strip along her back, a white patch at her waist, and that was all. She was poking through the cabinet again, pushing up on her toes. I wished she could not find her thing but would turn around and ask me where it is. She found it right away, but then stood there a hair too long, holding it. Then she turned toward the tub just enough I saw a big round white attached to the strip. The life sunk out of my face, but she turned back and sped out.

She called through the door, "Wring out those pants, and I'll iron them dry."

My cold went away as she spoke. I knotted the towel around my waist, opened the door a crack and hollered "Okay."

When she stomped up I was shoving the pants and underwear through the crack. A terrycloth robe came back. She said, "And do that nasty red shirt a yours and bring it to me."

The money went into the robe pocket. I found her in the living room creating so much steam ironing, the windows were beading. "I'd run the machine and do your clothes right if I wasn't running late."

She had switched outfits all right. A white skirt to her knees, with hundreds of tiny cotton balls, one every inch or so, tight at the ass, and a white blouse. She looked holy. Between the shirt buttons you could see a corner of the two round whites. While she pushed and pulled the iron her waist twisted as smooth as lake water. I felt very at home in a way I never had anywhere and could stay all afternoon and do whatever she asked. A perfume, a morning sweet not a nighttime bitter, floated in the humidity. So she had been rushing into that bathroom to flavor herself.

"I told you I didn't want to interrupt," I said.

"You didn't interrupt. I just have to be at work at the church in thirty minutes."

Most crackerjacks, you find, except Dad, are big believers. Most of them simply don't have time to wake up Sundays. Maybe Gawene got her religion juice by working a house of worship, and at more reasonable cluck hours, afternoon. Maybe she brought home some juice for the pocketbook as well.

She tossed me the pants and dug the iron into my underwear. I felt sort of personally violated, her going into my things. I usually wash and hang up my own. Here I'd watched her in hers, and I could watch her do whatever she wanted in this living room, but I did not even know what kind of work she did. And I had been hiding my money from her. I'd known the Stevenses, what, two years? And I didn't know them.

I put the nickel bag on that ironing board. She eyed it and kept working. "You don't need to," she said.

"I found it in my pocket."

With the ironed clothes I dressed in the bathroom. The pants pocket was still moist when I stuffed in the bucks, but so were the waist and cuffs and the velvet shirt. I found a comb to part my soggy hair, and that big old round head, more like a brown football on its side, I swear had lost an inch from right and left. It was more of a regular ball now. Some of that fold under the chin had gotten tucked. Walking too much and not eating enough must do their jobs. Mouth will always be small, but I could lose the downturn at the ends. If my nose would grow out, I wouldn't just be Chubby Chabney. The green eyes somehow gave my egg-brown tint a green I'd never seen. Hope it wasn't jaundice. Hope it all was signs of a new face coming out, with some boy charm, like those slick butterflies coming out of their sacs.

"You'd get a ride except Tim and Palla took the car," Gawene said at the door. She was studying me again. "You boys gonna fix that shower at home?"

I didn't answer right off, trying to keep up the mood. Walking off that porch felt good, like we would be doing this parting routine in reverse this evening, and so on every day.

"Our shower never worked so well," I said. "That was the best bath I ever had."

She only gave a very farewell wave, instead of the follow-up answer I needed, which was something like "That won't be

City Limit

the last best bath you ever had." So straightway as I came down
the Morrell hill past the houses boarded with plywood into the
Corinth valley, I saw only my carpet on High Hat ahead.

II.

13.

About an hour after dark that night in my High Hat basement, the door upstairs got a knock. I went up and asked who is it. A woman behind the door said she'd heard someone here was selling protection, and her brother needed a small hand-sized. I had crashed here only three nights, thought I was slipping in and out like a cat, and already the neighborhood knew my address. That's a fright.

I told her come back tomorrow night, then I dropped back downstairs and spun circles on my soggy carpet. I needed Dad's steel door, or at least a few more deadbolts. Gun dealers didn't get raided as much as crank dealers because most raiders were crackerjacks and feared the wrong kind of blast. Still I did not like how I was on the map as a place with a bankroll.

After about two hundred times around that carpet, I began slowing. That bankroll was in my pocket, warming my leg, and it was begging to grow and warm me up more. A big warm roll in the pocket had to be your most comfortable feeling, except for watching Gawene iron in her living room. And I'd learned, let the customers come to me.

But my new worry about the door knock kept me awake and wet and cold another night. Next morning, I stopped by the discount center for a backpack, then on to Husker Metcalf's. My cold was back, running down my lip. He was home boring some small barrels. He's a very large white man with a chest stiff as a tabletop which he turns along with his head as he looks around. His white gray beard spills down so neat I keep thinking it's a napkin. In the living room, or I guess that's what it was, he has metal lathe, metal drill press and sanders. It's the only place I've known that smells of pure metal. When I breathed I swear the air glittered with iron dust. He dug his way to the kitchen, or onetime kitchen, moving machinery aside as he went. Rows of crankshafts and barrels, pistol grips, revolver cylinders, tiny firing pins, cartridges, bolts and firing chambers filled the kitchen counters, except for a coffee pot. Dad once said Husker Metcalf had long choked his garage with broken machining tools. Since he designed his own weaponry, except an odd imitation Beretta .45 or Colt 30-30, I hardly recognized one item. All the merchandise looked like so many pies in a bakery window, I couldn't help myself, said fill my bag with one-fifty worth.

He dropped in a select item from here and there, like he was chasing me down the real bargains. I trusted they all worked since I could only guess how to sweeten them. "It's about time you get out and handle business on your own," he said. He had a high whiny voice that you might think was upbraiding someone. I had not said a word about my doing business on my own.

"Dad tell you I should do business on my own?"

On every trigger guard he'd knotted a string with a tag telling the caliber so customers would know what size bullet. Police had never busted him since there wasn't a rule against hobbyists.

"He didn't say."

Husker Metcalf was expert as me at saying things so you got your answer without getting what you wanted. I gave up and said, "So when did you last see him?" I was also learning I was good at giving myself away with the wrong questions.

"He came by for a comparable grabbag."

"Because he can't fix. Say anything else about me, like my fixing abilities?"

"Not that I recollect."

Husker Metcalf looked at me down that napkin tucked in his throat. I felt he saw into me, down to the night I left Dad's place. That bit about my doing business on my own, it sounded like he was looking out for my interests. But it also sounded like he was looking out for Dad's.

He dropped four pistols in the bag, which meant about $37.50 apiece. How could that amount pay for the bulk iron, much less his labor? Being the good businessman, I asked, "They all work?" Of course, with a look I'd soon enough see if they did.

He held a hand to the hall door that led to his basement. "Anyone's welcome to test." He had a padded room in his basement with targets set up, where Dad would sometimes go. I'm ashamed to say, but I'd never shot a gun. Dad wouldn't let me till I reached fourteen which he considered the legal shooting age. Though I could draw you enough ballistics charts to send the bullet home.

"No thanks. I think Dad tested you enough."

I then whiled my time buying a small Coleman stove and gas for heating. I figured I should load myself down only with enough objects to fill the pack, in case of sudden move-out. Under the lamp I read magazines I'd found dumped, up by the dog, mostly women's. They have useful stuff like how to quick-patch a tear in your shirt with nail polish or save money on gas by soaking dried beans first. There was plenty dumped nail polish up by the dog.

My customer lady didn't show until, must have been, nine or ten that night. She knocked me out of a good sleep. I went upstairs, and when I told her the price, sixty, she wanted two. She ran off for more cash. Here I thought I was milking her, with $22.50 profit for me per item, and she went bargain-crazy. Will I ever price myself right?

In the morning her brother-in-law came shopping. I gave him the wacky twelve-chamber revolver for eighty, and he made a stink. "You master rip-off!"

14.

In a couple days I sold off not just the four Husker Metcalfs but another set of three guns I bought on the street. I was running a sale down to somebody's cousin off Marsalis when an old fence of Dad's recognized me, near the lumberyard by Clarendon. He took me to his nightwatchman's box and showed a carton of broken Colt .22 Diamondback revolvers. "A feller found them in the dumpster, right out back, a month ago. Nobody wants them." Grips were split open, cylinders missing pins and loose as rocks, barrels rusted and triggers so clogged they were frozen. But he didn't see me glow. I felt I was copping him at sixty the set and was bilking myself since who would fix them but me?

I took three days in my basement, soaking beans and wearing out my eyes under the lamp. I buffed oil on rusted bores till they sparkled like porcelain, replaced screws the size of ant legs and wasted a day trying to carve my own firing pin cross pin from a paperclip. Finally I took the job up to Husker Metcalf, who lathed me the pin in ten seconds. Then I hiked my three gems up to Ray's on Singelton and came back with two-hundred forty more of a bulge in my pants.

It was time I found a stronger bank than my basement where the mice could gnaw profits. Till I sold the Husker Metcalfs I'd spent about everything I made, on burgers, supplies, shoes, stove, more guns. Then I'd gotten 290 for the Huskers, spent 60 for the Colts, brought in 240 for them, so I had close to 470 inside these dufflebags called pants. If High

Hat was like home back on Illinois, then every crank packed his iron but was free game, to be rolled for all he was worth. But the fella who sold gat, now, he was bathed in oil, no one laid hands on him, as if selling metal made you a crack shot. Sometimes, outdoors, my customers caught my eye. And one, the woman who I swore had bought to settle her marriage, tried a wave at me, that is until she seemed to recall who I was. I'd passed the three children who had raided me, and one pointed maybe a fake barrel at me through his coat, then they ran. There were the Dallas black-and-whites roaming High Hat every quarter hour, but they were only another color of passerby. Like hornets they only sting when they raid, and they only raid the rock houses. The big problem would be another set of children who didn't know me, or the same ones who got too playful.

So I swung by Oak Cliff Bank and started a genuine bankroll. The place smelled like a chilled version of the sweat that rolls off cash. My age pleased the lady. "It's good they start saving early, so they'll be set by the time they retire." She had a big pout and sunrays of wrinkles springing from her mouth. She gave me an inch of tissues for the cold dripping onto her desk. ID was a problem; I'd never had a bonafide birth certificate I'd known of. Dad had wormed me into school with some junk version he'd procured through his connections. But for passbook savings she and her homey place took my word I was eighteen. The address floored me because they would send letters showing the money. True, $150 was Dad's, plus about fifty for the confusion and maybe starvation I was causing him. But I was socking away about a hundred for my own trouble, and I didn't want him hauling that letter up here and taking my share. Luckily I recalled the numbers on Gawene Stevens's porch. So I had four weeks, before a statement got mailed, to think up an excuse and warn her.

When the bank lady reached out for my cash, instinct pulled the wad back to my belly. I said, "How do I know you'll give it to me when I ask?"

"The government guarantees we will, up to a hundred thousand dollars."

I sighed and felt empty walking out of that chilly place. But I bought a five gallon pail, filled it at a High Hat water hose and treated myself to my first home bath at the basement sink.

Give myself a week, at the rate I was going, and I could get us something better than that old Honda '78.

In a week I was lying on the swamp carpet of the first basement I'd occupied, staring at three unsold pieces. My cold was flooding my pipes, and I was coughing up something purple and green. I'd hack ten, fifteen minutes till my lungs about turned inside out, like some cancer riddled gick monsters of Dad's, and I didn't even smoke. One night, in my drier basement across the way, an old wino had slipped in with me and my key. I'd let him stay, in the bathroom. But the drift from his briefs of the past couple decades drove me to pack up at midnight and come to this other basement that was empty again. And he seemed to put a stink jinx on the three pieces I'd bought the day after my bank visit. Maybe my cold, my fake Keds, mold growing on me from the carpet or mice peeking out of my jacket, something was scaring away customers. I don't believe it was my fearsome rep. I had a weird mix of merchandise: Browning .22 target pistol, Smith & Wesson .45 and Remington deer rifle, from the lumberyard fence. They only needed the minor touching up I could do by day, since this hole lacked electricity. So much for my idea that customers would just come to me. I had stretched my walks to west of Beckley and north of Eighth. I slinked around the High Hat units till a Dallas black and white slowed for me. I tried poker with a mix of old men and preteens playing on oil drums and lost thirty bucks. I knocked at the few former customers' doors I knew and got only grumps behind shut wood. I even went back to Dad's old trick of buying boubou first, and I was only seven dimebags richer for it. I had no idea how to sell crack, since he rarely sold it. The time I'd come closest to trying the stuff was sniffing coke once; it just made my nose numb. Which might be useful for a diehard cold.

So here I was on my back, watching night come on my three wares and kill my reading. The wino was gone from the other basement, and I was giving one more day for his residue to clear, then moving back to the electricity. Or running back to Dad, with little more than what lay in the bank, no new cars.

The ceiling and its asbestos tiles all stained and falling gave me a glimpse of what lay ahead: weeks all tainted and broken like this past one. No more beginners' luck. I had used up the tiny supply of customers the world was allowing me.

At least, for a while before the end, I'd lose weight.

A few minutes before night, your eyes can't tell if it's arrived. That was just when a shadow hit the window.

It jockeyed about trying to get a good seat. Then it crouched. Then the body itself came into view. It was a short thin one, and in two seconds I pinned it. Dad.

At first I thought it was his ghost, except I don't believe in ghosts and ghosts don't leave shadows. But in the far-off front door light that made the shadow, his little craggy face just showed.

My heart hammered. I about cried out. Then his head moved around, angling on specks of light inside. I knew he was being cautious, but he looked sneaky. Why couldn't he have come for me all those daytimes I was hoofing the streets, instead of poking through a dangerous place he couldn't see?

He cupped his hands on the glass. I was far back, out of the light. At one point his glance nailed into me. I couldn't wave or peep but just wriggled under the nail. Then it struck me he hadn't come for me but for someone else, a customer or connection. So late at night? He had to be ragged to pieces, without my keeping the leash on him. His face looked the same, all I could tell. Maybe it was more caved in at those canyons down his cheeks. His eyes had sunk further down their craters. Or the backlighting put death in his face.

Then his glance fell off me and leapt around till it landed a spot way up close to the window. He was scowling so, that spot had to be what he had come to see, and all I saw there was carpet stain. I was so busy guessing what he hunted for and fearing he'd scoot if I ran to the window, I forgot to make a plan of contact. It took him only two more seconds to shake his head, push to his feet and fly.

For the next few seconds I was waiting for his knock at the upstairs door. Those seconds bled away. A panic seemed to hit my ears, and I ran upstairs as fast as my heavy ass let me. The puling deadbolt fussed with my hands several minutes for the first time ever, and I jumped through the door and stood there.

City Limit

The bulbs by the units' front doors burned cold yellow. The walks were empty. Far off a cat hollered mating. The tree limbs rubbed each other in a breeze.

I still did not believe in ghosts. But after a short time looking for him, I went in and shut the deadbolt in one snap. I saw no other explanation. I lay on the carpet, but most of the night I got up and paced.

15.

When I finally made my way outside late that morning, the army of water heaters was gone. The only signs they had ever stood were bits of piping and the holes their toes left. It felt as if Dad had been the taker and had peeped on me only as a sidetrip. But that yard with its ghosts of the cylinders woke me to daylight: No ghost had visited.

Later a neighbor said the city's special large-garbage truck had come early in the morning. Someone had long copped a few bucks' of copper tubing.

That day I determined I had to go to Dad's, if only visit, check on him, look at his door till he came out on two feet and not crawling.

As soon as I got rid of these puling last three pieces.

Tired as my feet were from a night of pacing, they pushed me and my sales pitch to the edges of Oak Cliff. Actually into the riverbottoms itself. In a clearing of the marsh reeds two white suburb brothers target-practicing with .22s took the Smith & Wesson. The same panic in my gut, like last night's when Dad fled my window, drove me to walk up to anybody who showed highbeams and offer the dimebags I'd bought. Dad's ghost glances stayed in the corner of my eyes, so I only had to blink and there he was. Why did he run away from me after I had run away from him?

Had I seen him?

The dimebags sold me into the graces of a dentured old gentleman with a cane who wanted pocket protection. A girl of about thirteen who didn't have breasts yet bought the deer rifle. I would never have walked up to such a girl before that day, and she was about the tenth such girl I tried since morning, mostly like a joke. But this one opened her red plastic Catwoman purse, took out eighty and put the Remington in her coat.

By that night, I had shaken off all the dimebags and pieces. I was back in my dry cellar with my lamp and magazines. All I could tell myself was, last night's visitor must have scared the luck into me. Next morning I got up to set off for burgers, then bank, then the old Illinois Avenue home.

And I was buttoning my shirt to go when I got another visitor. I swore I knew that knock, pounding just like codes on our old door. In fact, was that a $- \cdot - - \cdot$ for "Gullo"? Back in my days at Illinois, when Dad had gone out leaving me alone then returned and knocked the code, his knuckles used to make only a bird tap.

I went up and asked who's there, my voice cracking because I already knew. "Hey, I did get the right place," said the voice. "The round dude."

The voice sounded cheery as usual. Why was that guy chasing me down way over here? Must have bad news. Dad had been hauled off crack-crazy after all. Or my messenger himself had dispatched him. To Laurel Land.

The deadbolt fucked with my fingers again. Door opened on Rick Ocotillo, gray suit black shirt black tie and blindfold shades against that winter gray sky. "Man, you lose weight? You're down to an oversized football," he said.

I never knew what to say to our landlord. He gazed around at the smudgy yellow walls of my staircase. "See you got yourself set up like home. The city has a lot of patience with this street and won't go away and let a fair manager come in. So you doing those lovely codes like Daddy used to? Hell, I threw in what I remembered, just in case, I figured you'd keep the old ways, want to know who is legit. And look, it worked."

I did not like the way he spoke of Dad in terms of "used to" and "remembered." He stopped nosing in my stairwell where his shades couldn't see anyway and pouted and turned his chin to the tree branches. "If you don't want to invite me in for old times, I'll just hang here wicha a minute. Hey, I broughtcha something." He reached into his jacket and pulled out a small box with a celluloid window and gave it to me. It was a DL&W Mother Hubbard 2-6-0 locomotive and tender, HO scale. "I searched for that one," he said. "It'll get you started." I held it, staring not in awe but wondering what do I say to a guy who doesn't know my urges.

"Dang, dude, you don't got Dad here to do the talking anymore," he said. "How you feed yourself if you don't chat up customers? You just hold up the number of fingers in ten dollar amounts? Maybe that's why the ball's losing the air. Anyway, I won't keep you from your hobbies. I just wanted to drop by as old friends of your Dad—and of you too, I thought. And let you know there's already a man on my bomb squad covering this street's bullion. You can keep your rock indoors or take it to the riverbottoms. I suggest you speak to my man when he knocks, add some hamburger helper to your meal ticket. I'm starting to look after the people up here, in the units the city's seemed to have forgot."

He had to know about Dad and wasn't telling me, and this was all I could read from him. But I didn't want to say a word about Dad and give myself away as I always did when I talked, in case Dad was alive and okay and word got back what I was saying. I said, "I don't need protection."

Rick Ocotillo has thin lips, and they pucker up to a kiss when he smiles. "Of course you don't, you're a Gullo. But your customers need it, if you can find any."

"You won't send me them?"

"Don't need to. Another man on this street's keeps them happy. Hey, my dude's talking to me!"

"I haven't seen any man." No wonder I'd had no more luck on High Hat and had to scout far and wide to make a sale. "Dad used to sell here."

"Try opening them eyelids. Every day changes. Look for a place of your own."

He moved away at that easy pace of his, like the camel at Marsalis zoo. He wasn't even Spanish, just some Ukrainian or something, named himself after cactus. He had not given me a thing I'd needed. "How come I need hamburger helper if I can't get customers?"

"I'm just sharing facts as an old friend. I don't traffic in advice."

As he ambled down the walk I saw a pipeline to Dad clamp shut. But Rick Ocotillo was the last pipeline I'd want carrying bits about me to Dad. You had to claw through all the fat that Rick Ocotillo spewed to find the meat.

Instead of rushing on to Illinois, I slid back downstairs and sat on the carpet. Rick Ocotillo made you want to stay indoors and quiet. He seemed to set a rule against every move you could make, but you couldn't state the rule. I could not believe another man on High Hat sold pieces. No one had mentioned him all the times I tried selling here. But how could Rick Ocotillo guess I had hit a wall here?

All I could make of the visit was: He had put Dad in Laurel Land, and he had come to see if I could fill in the hole Dad had left

Starving, I had only a dusty sack of beans from my poor days and had to soak them. If I could not get back into Dad's place, I had to get a car. I'd be fourteen in a couple months, but enough folks took me for sixteen or so, I could drive safe enough without a license. A car was my only place to do business, only place to set up house.

16.

For a couple weeks I got out of that basement at dawn and stayed out till night. Not that nighttime in the basement was safer, but coming and going in sunlight was worse. During the day I gave High Hat a mile clearance. I stopped by Husker Metcalf's for wares. He was running out of cheapo oddballs and started dropping more premium morsels in my sack. They cut into my margin, since a fatboy in the street, without a lovely glass display case, couldn't command Ray's Sporting Goods prices. When I suggested a more attractive pricetag, the customer did turn my offer from front to back before sneering and handing it back. At least a Husker Metcalf did not ask for much oil and screw-driving. When the man ran dry of all but high-end, I fell back on the nightwatchman fence, and he passed me to another fence who janitored up at Cliff Temple Baptist. And that fence landed me another contact, and soon I got a cell and saved on walking. No one, even Husker Metcalf, offered news of Dad.

It makes me crazy how you can go long times with nothing happening except business or no business, but no personal visits. Then out of nowhere you get visits and swear your life is about to turn inside out. Then those fizzle away too, and it's back to another stretch of business or no business.

For customers, I scraped up old ones by falling by their homes. You risk seeing an eye of a barrel behind the door for having sold someone a jammed chamber. But I trusted my handiwork, and if they wanted to blast me for their inability with the goods, at least my feet would stop aching. Most of the conversations came through shut doors. What else could I say but something silly? "I just wanted to see if that piece I sold is holding up." "Who knows if it holds up? I ain't shooting nobody to test it. Whatta you doing asking?" Sometimes they open up, and we chat about their flower beds or the Dallas Cowboys. One or two buy another piece because they like my prices, but some tell me of a cousin or aunt looking. And then those cousins or aunts have a cousin or aunt. I don't know why I was so scared, to the point I was working myself so hard. It sure beat the dry spell of a while back. At the end of every week, I was also falling by the bank.

Each time, the teller told me they could not hand over that letter coming to me. It was sent from a machine far away. That time when Gawene Stevens would get it was creeping up. Much as I'd love another bath at her house, if only she'd come in digging for her perfume again, more likely Palla or Tim Stevens would answer my knock. I might be able to walk up to a stranger's door to sell a converted M-16, but not to Gawene Stevens's to ask for my own envelope. But none of those strangers wore a tight white skirt with hundreds of tiny cotton balls on it.

It was a Friday night when another knock came upstairs. Since my last visitor, only one customer had stirred me from my magazines at night for a purchase. But I can tell a customer's mousy tap. This was that heavy fist again, and then the $- \cdot - - \cdot$.

I lay still. But I was by my lamp that was in view of the window. Couldn't shut it off because the shutoff would show through outside. I pushed up and stepped across the carpet, taking my sack with its sawed-off and two pistols. Against the wall by the window, I took out the sawed off. I had no shells as usual, stupid scaredy-cat me. The knocks turned into arm slams, then the full body a few times. That puny deadbolt I'd screwed on and off myself when changing basements was all that held that door. I aimed the sawed-off at the staircase door.

The voice came from outside through the ceiling. "Hey, round dude!" Soon steps came to the window, and the voice again. Luckily the window had those bars. Out of sight of the window I was holding the sawed-off close. A heel hit the bars with a metal thud.

A good half hour after his footsteps disappeared, I turned off the lamp. Two visits, Rick Ocotillo was trying to tell me something. I waited another quarter hour, then stuffed the valuables into the backpack, all few of them, including the model train that should fetch something. I peeked out the door. The units were noisy with a cold March wind, which didn't stop the usual Friday night ruckus. People still kept windows open, to let out all the bickering televisions and puling brats and rap. The wind was just the ice cream to carry the chips of noise. Folks shouted from one unit to other, two units away, I think just to make themselves heard. Small crowd, smaller than usual, bantered around an oil drum, close, trying to block the wind from the cards that they held down with fingers. You could disappear safer in a choked Friday night than in a dead calm sunrise. My landlord might be visiting other sheep here, but I could avoid High Hat and slip the back way to an alley and up to Hutchins St. I had to get over my scare that Dad was dead and go find out.

Hutchins kept me safe, with the same Friday hullabaloo pouring out the small houses and the cars parked out front. Since the houses were wide apart with more sky, you felt less caged in. People leaning on fenders nodded at you like neighbors or scowled guessing what's under your jacket. At Cedar Crest I cut down to Bonnie View. It wound me past the golf course and the woods across the street, both so dark and still that you felt anything could leap out. It seemed a year, or longer, long ago as my childhood, since that rainy night I'd staked out across the golf course. I hadn't done that many more things than when I was with Dad, I had just done them without him. I went through the storm sewer pipe again and missed the crunchy tortillas with Tonio. In the William Brown Miller playing fields, I stopped. There were small kids down in the creek, the lighters for their boubou showing in the dark, and it was like old times, when I was a kid. Their laughs and grunts in the trees were the only sound except the wind over the field and the faroff traffic down Illinois. A whiff of their fumes blew up, that smell of plastic and sugar, like off Dad's pipe. I hated the stuff but loved the smell.

I forced my puling feet to move on. I had to know if he needed me. I cut across Bonnie View and along the path through the woods. The trees whistled with that chilly wind. Winos were smart enough not to start fires in the woods tonight. Long before Spanish Fort, I took a cutoff to the shopping strip. Funny how half a lifetime later you recall the paths through the trees, eyes closed. Then I was coming over the rise in the broken pavement before the strip. I stopped in the shadows between lampposts. There was our unit, the board over the door and the door through the board. And from Dad's spot in front, the '78 Honda was gone.

City Limit

Of course, Friday night, he made it to the base houses for some bazooka and business. I'd just never stood here watching the empty space of asphalt under the orange street light. That orange glow can make a place look empty. Usually I'd be with him, or locked in the basement with some magazines, depending on if he was at a thirst monster's or at an average beamer's.

So, I'd wait a little. He'd be back anytime.

As the night passed I would shuffle all the way over to Spanish Fort and stare across the street awhile. That boarded door, I'd remember, long time ago didn't have the board but was black with a brass number sixteen for our unit. I used to think of that sixteen as the future when I'd be an adult and could drive, though even at seven Dad sat me in his lap and let me wheel. Back then men mowed the patches of grass between the dirt, but now the grass looked like bushes edging the units.

I slunk back into the shadows in the parking lot and toed at the trash in the craters. The lot was mostly potholes with some skinny flat tar-patches snaking through. I found a kid's cap gun, all metal, loaded with a rain damaged coil of caps. It looked like a real .22 Colt revolver. Maybe the kid was buried under the trash, and this was his last holdout. Way down the coil were some good caps, and I fired a couple, with a big flash and echo against the store fronts. This piece could hold you out well in some situations. I thought of Rick Ocotillo barging down my stairs. But you didn't know which situations. I still needed to fire a real one.

The few cars turning down Spanish Fort off Illinois swept headlights across the lot or across the units. I would watch it even when the headlights were too halogen white or fog-lamp yellow or wide apart to be the Honda. Just in case he got a new car. Let's say, another car, don't say new. But the car pulled into another unit's space or trickled on down Spanish Fort or swung into the lot and did business there then drove on.

It felt like dawn was coming, and I sat slouched against a lamppost. It was time to go home, to my High Hat basement I mean. I was so worn from the inside of my eyes out, I could escape my head only in sleep.

So my chin was hitting my collar when a faroff car door clicked shut. My eyes flickered open, and way off past my shoes I saw a man leave a car. In the dark it appeared to be a Honda. I pushed to my feet and, staying out of shadows, pushed my sleepy ass over the craters. He was walking right to our unit.

Dad was.

But then before Spanish Fort, I stopped. He was ambling on, at a healthy pace, like he didn't have a clue I was anywhere around, I mean anywhere on the planet.

He went right to the boarded door, unlocked, opened and slipped in. I stood there angry, without a clue why. I felt like running up and pounding the door. But I didn't. He was perfectly well alive without me, not a drag to his walk like me and my sore heels tugging in these fake Keds. How was he fixing wares with his boubou bumbling fingers? He had to have found some sources better than Husker Metcalf and Harran's. And out of those mazes of roads twisting through Oak Cliff he knew, he could probably find plenty without me. How dare he.

Even when I crawled back to Hutchins and then High Hat, dawn still had not come. I'd passed a gas station clock showing 3:20. Friday night had slowed down, except for a roaring engine or two. I only wanted a peek at my basement window: Door and window bars were intact. But I still wasn't laying my neck on that carpet. I lugged my valuables up one more hill, the dog's. And there I stayed the next several nights.

17.

Back in the basement only a couple days, I got another visitor.

The tap came right at dark, around seven. Rick Ocotillo's visit had been around the same time of night. This tap was light, scared even, and I kept waiting for the – · – – ·. He had to be disguising his knock. My pack held a 30-30 magnum and two other pieces. Grabbing the pack I took the stairs barefoot. They squeaked more than I'd ever noticed. About the time I stopped at the door the tap sounded again. You can hear a lot through a shut door, and just behind it was some rustling of clothing, nylon. The Face had switched fabric? Then came some anxious throat noises or impatient grunts. Sounded female. Of course I thought Gawene Stevens, that soft knuckle knock, except she had no idea where I was. More likely, that same customer who likes to show up at my door, now becoming a regular. Still I held my breath when I stuck my ear to the wood. With that customer I should have started a code.

There was a high impatient sigh that had to be a woman's and clicks on the door that had to be long nails. Anyway I disguised my voice deep as I could and said who's there.

"That you, Chabney?" It was Gawene Stevens's chirpy voice.

I opened, and there stood Gawene Stevens with a hand on hip and hip pushed out. My first grade teacher used to take that pose when the class got noisy. "I don't see how anybody can open up without a peephole," she said. I almost hugged her, if only I did that kind of thing.

"I heard your fingernails," I said. Hers were long and purple with sparkles. "I get so I can hear the color of folks' shoes behind doors."

She was digging in her purse. "Don't tell me no dogshit like hearing the color of something, or I won't give you what I was gonna." She stopped digging and looked at my pack in hand. "You were just going out?"

"Just cleaning up, sort of."

She gawked at my stairwell, then at me, shaking her head like she'd changed her mind about why she'd come. "You really living here, Chabney? I'd heard tell, but you're really in this place. What you doing here? What you do with your Dad?"

"He's okay."

"Y'all didn't have a big fight? He wasn't doing nothing mischievous to you?" She said mischievous Miss Cheevious, which sounded really gnarled and painful.

"We're just branching out business."

"I knew you had a reason to come knocking for a shower, and you weren't telling me a thing. And I'm mad you'd lie at me, not saying what's what, and there I'd washed your clothes."

"I didn't lie, and I was the one washed my clothes. I just didn't know what the plan was with me and Dad then, so I didn't say." Here my tongue hadn't given myself away, but everyone else had. Even Gawene Stevens could find her way to me.

She gave the purse a last try and pulled out the envelope. "And I don't know what you're doing getting bank letters, and them coming to my house. Unless you been holding up banks and they want it all back. Don't put my home in the crossfire no more. Look how when you come over I take you in, and here you just stand in the door."

She handed me the letter, and I kept standing in the door because she had a real house with furniture and an ironing board and I just had carpet. She didn't mind me, though, and stepped right past. She was pushing her weight around because she was older, about nineteen or twenty Dad had said. Her generous skirt brushed me, and she left a whiff of violet and orange. "You don't have a light down these stairs, Chabney?"

I stood there, heart pounding, hoping she wouldn't take one more step down. But the nylon kept swishing, had to be the hose at her thighs, and the heels clonking wood. I tried, "There's nothing to see."

"There's steps to see, if I don't want to smash my nose." She hit the bottom. "Okay, I see light through a door, so don't tell me about electricity shortage."

Heart pounding so bad I stuck a hand at my chest, I took a step down. It was too much, how she was in my place and in the dark in my place, but it would be worse in the light because I would see what she was wearing. Then she pushed open the door, and there in the light was her profile, short nose and high cheeks and strong jaw like statues they find on the Nile River.

"Gawene—" I stopped speaking because I had never said her name aloud and it sounded too personal to say. "Really, there's nothing. I just sleep here." She kept her profile in the door, gazing in. I had never seen her lit at that angle, hair pulled behind, and she was like another person from the purple haired lipsticked woman I'd seen.

"Lord, Lord, you don't have nothing, that's right." She slipped on inside. I came on down, one step at a time. I wished she would exit. When I looked through the hall door, she was strutting about glancing up at the walls and gouged-out kitchen like I had paintings and copper pans hanging. I had papered over the window and stuffed the niche between the bars with bricks and cloth so light couldn't go out. So I had to keep a lamp burning, and with the puling old circuits in the unit, the bulbs burned out in a day or two so I had bought a pile of bulbs stashed by the window. She gazed at them a while, probably for something real to give the eyes.

Her black skirt to the knees was a satin cloth you find in women's head scarves. It had a puffy lightness like skin, and turquoise and gold curlicues scattering through it. It hugged the ass. Under her thin jacket the turquoise top was slit open some, between buttons.

She turned at me, hands on the back of the hips, with a big face of pity and fright. I was expecting the mouth to pour out buckshot at me and my place. Instead she said, "Maybe it's worth it having a spot like this."

"And not a house like yours?" She had to be laughing at me.

"Tim's got threats against his life. A note said 'Get out,'' that's all. Two nights ago a bullet went right through the front door. He hadn't done nothing, Chabney. You know Tim. He just does his stuff, mows his lawns, helps Mom sell a few pieces. I never known anyone more peaceful. Somebody seen our house and wants it, is all. I know who it is, I'm sure of it, boy skeeger, a real chaser always doing bumps. He'd sell you perps and beat vials. Tim never took a thing, and this skeeger'd always go off sore. Man I hated that nasty puller, always squeezing his own cheeks. Palla took the baby off to Waxahachie. Tim doesn't know what to do but he's staying on. And I got my job."

I put the pack with my three pieces in it onto the kitchen counter without letting the contents clank and crammed the envelope inside to get it out of my sight. It seemed that asking myself into her house for a bath and stealing her address for a bank letter had set off all these bad things there. Maybe that skeeger saw my bank letter in the box and thought he could extort the Stevenses. Except he would have taken the letter and gone for my cash.

I said, "I didn't mean to make it hard on you."

She blinked. Her eyes had aquamarine around them, and I wondered a second if she had gone to work at church this way and just come back. The color looked like shock. "Chabney, what are you saying? And you don't do boubou. You think I'm saying you're the cause for anything?"

Then her face changed, the shock went out of the aquamarine and she came at me. Her lips were pouting. I backed a step, but then her cheek was against mine, it was wet even. She was a little taller than me, not as tall as her tall sibs. But I didn't want the hug because it was like a grown-up to a kid. "Poor Chabney. How could Arn leave you?"

The violet-and-orange was potent at this range. I stepped back again. She kept her hands on my shoulders. Her arms up, that slit between the buttons yawned. I kept thinking at her, Don't act like the adult.

"He didn't leave me," I said. "I left."

The fright came back to her face like now she'd pour buckshot. Her lips puckered, and out came only, "Wow." Her eyes switched left and right and down, all over my face, maybe hunting for dirt spots. That blue green was calm, up close, like those ad photos of beach oceans. She whispered, "He didn't do nothing to you?"

"Nothing." I spoke normal voice, awkward about the whispers. "Nothing at all."

We were silent so long, I finally craned around, jittering my shoulders. She dropped her hands, and I regretted my jittering and my blabbing how I had left.

"I'd thought Arn Gullo was so kind," she said.

"He is."

"Did he agree you could go? I can't imagine."

I took a long time. She might find out the opposite, but now it felt good to say, "Yes."

In a few minutes she pulled her jacket around her.

"You sleep on these blankets on the floor?" I nodded. She shook her head. "You got to do something about that."

She buttoned a couple of the top buttons and bundled away the slit.

"You can let those letters keep coming at me. You have an actual bank, Chabney Gullo? Not holding them up?"

"Yes."

Then she was clopping out the hall door and up the dark steps. I stayed right behind. I said, "You can't go back to that house."

"It'll be okay. Don't believe a skeeger blowing it out his ass."

And she opened the deadbolt herself, then I was watching her and the skirt fabric floating away until she bent around the last unit and disappeared down hill.

18.

That night on the carpet I switched from my left to right to back, picturing how this basement could look like a house. A bed and dresser, a kitchen table, curtains with sunlight through the window, ironing board. When I got to the sunlight through the window, I switched sides. No sunlight, no table, no dresser, no bed. I had to be ready to move out on a finger snap.

I scolded myself anyway, I shouldn't have let her run out. I could have promised I would install a steel hatch door. It would make her a better life than being exposed up there in the open, that is at her house.

The weeks swallowed me. Work stole me from the basement mornings and spat me back down the stairs at dark. No sunlight through my window to tell time, I found a clock. One picture in my head led me along, a house I could rent myself and not creep around some fake landlord. At the least, a car, which could be my own mobile bedroom. Since Rick Ocotillo had invited himself back into my life, I bought and sold anywhere just to snub him, including the High Hat units. I even bought a dimebag or two from a High Hatter to fuel sales-talk about my wares. And I sold the damn dimebags back to High Hatters. I wondered if back there at Illinois I hadn't left Rick Ocotillo more than I had left Dad. Nights, I kept switching left to right, waiting for the knock.

A timid knock came, twice. Again, I went up barefoot, pack in hand. Rick Ocotillo or Gawene Stevens? I hated to put my ear against the door in case my noisy blood vessels thudded it. I was breathing hard and about to choke on phlegm. The tap lacked the long purple nails. No whimpering throat outside, no heavy shoe steps. Had to be a customer. I let it go, both times.

Then on another night, I was actually asleep, and a boom woke me. A split second later rain slapped the outside wall upstairs, like that storm that hit the doghouse my first day there. It took me a moment to rouse and blink. That couldn't have been thunder and rain. That was fire and buckshot, on my front door.

I crouched till dawn, with all I would be carrying along gathered at my feet. When I creaked open the front door, dozens of holes decorated it and the wood and asbestos around it. A couple pellets that must have hit brick had rolled down the walk.

The Trinity riverbottoms called.

19.

Most of the bodies show up between the Corinth and Commerce bridges, in the mesquite flats on both river banks. I can't say just why. Maybe the access roads over the levy there from the south or from the cheap bars downtown on the north are convenient for a quick job. Winos and other derelicts avoid the area's reputation, so you could have some privacy. I found a patch of high mesquite that shaded me from the Thornton bridge, about fifty feet back from the ugly gray Trinity banks. If every few weeks someone were to drive past to unload their job from the trunk, I wouldn't mind, they'd be too busy to talk with me. Just so the dumper or the dumped wasn't one of my former customers and embarrass me.

Still, I set up camp for rapid departure. Under a big oak I laid out my blankets and stove. My sack, packed for sudden departure, stood upright against the trunk. The air was warming fast with spring and the rains were getting worse. The Trinity was skinny enough a good car could leap it. But there's a reason they built fifty-foot levies half a mile on either side. Every couple years, the water almost tops them and takes out a few poverty neighborhoods downstream. It tends to rise in minutes. Right across it were the green and black glass boxes of downtown. At night I counted computer screens, blue stars inside the windows. The outside stripes of skyscraper lights made big wrapped gift cartons.

I lit the stove only in the mornings, not to let my fire show to the bridge traffic like the wino fires used to show in the trees near home. I cooked the beans I'd soaked all night, threw them in a Tupperware box I'd found and nibbled all day, walking and working. Everything had to come along in the pack for the day's rounds. All this walking, I was losing weight fast and kind of missed it, like I was losing myself. I tried to stop once a day by Burger Mecca, to keep in shape. My reflection in Burger Mecca's glass showed some baggy clothes. I looked like one of those posts in the river that collects the branches and litter. Maybe a pretty thick post. So I always treated myself, to a double with double fries. You have to look healthy for customers. And the clothes had to tumble in the laundromat every few days, both changes, while I stood by in tee and boxers. Fatboys, even ones losing their fat status, can't fuss with briefs. At a park spigot, the Keds lookalikes got a good rinsing off of the riverbottom sludge. All I needed was an iron.

The real trick was getting a working car. I could not spend half a day on gun maintenance in Kidd Springs Park then bolt away when the phone called me to a meeting, but then have to stop and spend a half a day praying over a carburetor. Who would sell a fourteen-year-old a car, when title and insurance spell the ID game?

My janitor fence at the Baptist church was running dry. Besides, Gawene Stevens worked in the office around front, and I so badly wanted to run into her I was afraid I would. He gave me another source, a man who bought and sold aboveboard but seemed too old to see what I was. This man lived in an aluminum shed behind a transmission and radiator shop, with a gravel yard. He had a bunk, the same gas stove as mine, parts of pistols everywhere else and his arms dealers license on the door. The bare bulb hung from a string knotted with Pez heads. The place reeked of radiator fluid till you choked, and you tramped the green stuff everywhere. The gray hairs on his head stood up about six inches. When I held out cash he saw so poorly he reached a half a foot to my left. But he could always dip a hand into that swamp of pistol parts and fish up a complete working piece.

"Don't let truck drivers get a hold of it," he warned. "They'll blow you off the road." I went to him a lot because he was easy and said his goods weren't stolen. Sometimes you want a break from stolen property. But I think I was his only customer. The swamp of parts looked the same five days later.

Every day, Gawene Stevens sat at my shoulder. I could feel the fright or pity on her face without turning around to look. "Don't just walk up to that skeeger in the shades," she scolded, "his type think they can out-ass fatboy and'll blast him if he wins." "Who are you, bowing down to no piper," I'd scold back, "I have to sell to whoever, if we're getting anywhere." It's easy to scold someone on your shoulder.

The time came around to stop by her house for the next bank letter. Then it passed. I imagined that skeeger who Tim Stevens knew finding the letter in her box. All my bank notices coming to the Stevenses' could rile that skeeger up till he threatened her too. Maybe I was ridiculous to think my bank letters in her box could inspire his threats. It'd seem too waggy to ask her go get me a P.O. box. She must have had a bank too since she had a church job. But I did have to stop my letters coming or go get them before she took them for a walk and discovered my basement was empty or a wino answered her knocks. Still I could not bring myself to go stand on her porch again.

City Limit

Staying at the riverbottoms kept me far from another person, Dad. The walk back from Illinois was too long to do at night, and I still could not go show my face around there by day. Of course I might try to make the hike at nightfall and camp in the trees off Bonnie View. But every evening I slouched to my mesquite flats and collapsed.

Then, me and my walking pack everywhere, the one whom they call The Man spied me one time too many.

20.

Every afternoon since I'd come to the riverbottoms, the heat built up fast as the clouds. My pack's shoulder straps squeezed the water out of my chest and rubbed it raw. The clouds went black, and around five they'd flash and blow up. I'd find a shed or fallen-down sign for the hour or two of water dump. Mornings I'd wake to a Trinity ten feet closer to my body, so nights I was dropping myself twenty feet closer to the levy.

So, around five o'clock, I'd just made a sale off Du Bois near Avenue L and was slogging back up 11th. The clouds were green and brown and twirling. Cartons drove sloppy with the wind down the street. The corner of my eye caught another big box trailing alongside me. Then a nosey sounding loudspeaker told me halt.

Doors of a Dallas black and white swung open. Two big guys got out, holsters and batons at their belts. They told me they had seen me walking around too many days with this backpack. Since I wore it like an article of clothing they were going to frisk it and my pants. To frisk the pack properly, they had to sink their hands in deep.

For a few seconds I was fearing for a semi-automatic Uzi I had converted to automatic. First time in my life I was stopped, all those years with Dad. He was so good at looking good, even in that Honda. But my fear was leaping ahead of me. I'd sold the Uzi earlier this afternoon. The last piece of the set, a Beretta, had gone only twenty minutes ago.

Dad's luck was with me today.

Done with my pack, the cops stood tall and uncomfortable. They only found a stove, blanket, cell phone, a change of clothes, my fixit kit. Apparently they didn't repair their own heat and recognize my tools. They asked why I was hauling the pack around town so much by foot. I said, "Friends."

They gave a look with steel chins. The warning drilled into me. Their boots clomped onto the squad car floor and the doors slammed.

The rain was chasing me as I picked up to a run along 11th. I was so lucky, had sold my last piece, just in time, the rain felt fresh and cool after the day. No reason to take shelter. And as I came around 11th at East 8th, three kids were beelining across the bald lawn of Moore Park. We were on collision course, on the sidewalk ahead. The rain was pounding, globs hard as pellets, but it felt good as slaps on the back. Then the kids seemed to speed up to ensure that collision, so fast the smallest was screeching slow down.

Instead of colliding, they stopped in time for one to hold out the stub barrel of a sawed-off at me. The rain was so heavy now that while the kid had the whole thing out of his coat nobody five feet away could have seen. Though no one was outside anyway. I saw enough to notice it was a Remington, and it looked familiar. In these three kids, I saw the ones I'd sold the same Remington months ago.

"Give me what you got," said the ten-year-old. These kinds of kids, they have no problem emptying a chamber, it's just a cap gun. Since they were patting me down, I emptied my pockets of the $468 of the past few days' till. I was ready for the rest of my life to go next. But they passed up the boring looking bank letter all rain-destroyed in my pocket. They asked for the pack and got upset I only had peppermints. The ten-year-old, the spokesman, threw them down and stomped on them. "Why don't you got no Xtreme Sour Berry Pop Rocks?" he said. He handed the gun to the twelve-year-old, dumped my sack on the sidewalk and ripped my change of shirt. But he stuffed the rest of my things back in the sack and hefted it onto his shoulder. They did not appear to recognize me as their arms dealer. Or maybe they did and had no time to say hello.

The ten-year-old took the gun back, finger going to the trigger. He pointed, not aimed, somewhere between me and the eight-year-old, but he was trying to get that barrel on me. But first there came an orange white swell of light from that black hole. And then the explosion. It blended in with the thunder. I could hardly see after that flash. But even over the rain I heard metal bits hitting metal signs and cars. A sawed-off blows so wide, I was probably just out of the spray. The ten-year-old was thrown onto his back, then he was up and the three were running, screaming. Through blinks of flash and rain blinding me, I made out the eight-year-old was holding his side.

It took minutes till I moved along, where I'd been headed, up 11th, as if I'd only stopped and scratched a bad sore. The streets were empty except for the rain hitting the new rivers. I'd never seen anything like that orange white light. My ears were booming from the boom in my ears. I was shaking so bad, I only now noticed the temperature had dived ten degrees in ten minutes. If only those cops hadn't stopped me, I would have been way ahead of those kids. What puling luck.

I was starting to shake, couldn't move. That orange white light stayed in my eyes, bluegreen now. Now I smelled the powder. Either he'd had only one shell or his finger had not pulled a second time, when that barrel would have swerved right to me.

I came back to the High Hat basement as if I'd never left it for the riverbottoms. Without blankets I had nowhere else. The kids did not take the key or some coins in my pocket. That key went into my old deadbolt lock, and the air of must pouring out the door was stronger than the rain. Miracle, the pellet holes in the door must have scared off the winos. I went down and lay on nothing.

21.

The rain smashed the earth all night. When it stopped, I woke with the shock of something missing. I also felt refreshed, like you do some time after a bad gash in the leg, and then your body gets this warm feeling. Yesterday's bluegreen flash still traveled around the eyes.

I lay awhile, satisfied I still had one thing, that bank. And, I swear, I wasn't ten hours back in this pit, when the knocks came. But at once I knew that knock. This time I had no protection or anything else to carry upstairs with me. I ran up barefoot, and as I pulled at the deadbolt I guessed that those pellet holes would come asking for their payment. Rick Ocotillo would send about anyone to take care of such basics. I was ready to give up the chase; I was cornered. So I threw the deadbolt, and on my doorstep in the blue morning was Gawene Stevens.

"Chabney!" she shrieked way too loud for the neighbors. And she dropped on me, all her arms going around my back. We stayed that way awhile, wrapped up, or I guess I held on, I didn't know what to do when a person did such a thing. The way she gripped and smelled of spice and blossom perfume, I didn't seem like some relative. "I'd heard you were staying at the riverbottoms."

"Who told you that?" I had to pull back, much as I didn't want to but felt I should. "So why'd you come here?"

"And these bullet holes, Chabney. Don't tell me it's you they're firing at. I don't know what you're doing here, but man I'm glad to find you here." She took me back into the wraparound. The day was chilly and damp but she had no jacket, just the shirt, one like the last I'd seen her in, the cloth you see in headscarves, the feel of skin. Her topside pressed into me, and I stayed very still, very conscious of them soft and hard against me.

I had to repeat myself. "I don't see why you came here."

"You never have a radio or television. That's gonna get you in trouble some day."

Dad couldn't have been the one who told her about me camping out, unless someone had told him. I had only peeped to the old man behind the transmission shop, because he'd asked about the dried grass on my pack. "Is the radio telling where I'm sleeping?"

"It's telling where you better not. Were you at the river, Chabney?" Now she was pulling back, to make sure I answered true. I was getting embarrassed, us in the door with our noses almost touching, so I scooted inside. I tried to keep us together so I could feel her soft and hard against me. But she was standing apart and stern.

"For a while," I said.

"And last night was the first you were here, I'm sure of it. Because I was checking every night I could get away, couple times a week. And you were stirring me up again, Chabney, still not telling me nothing. Because these damn bank letters coming at me, you got me looking after you. I didn't ask for them, you just hook me into it and go off leaving me cold. I know what responsibility is, but you sure don't."

She was so angry at me, like no one had ever been, after she had been so gushy. She could have damn well called me if she'd only asked for my number last time. I toed the door shut. It was dark now and I didn't have to look at her anger, but I knew I should have gone and gotten those letters and I felt awful. "Did the skeeger come again?"

"Which skeeger? The one in front of me sure didn't." Then, in the dark, she swallowed me up in herself again. The odor was so strong in the dark I saw color patterns, orange and blue curlicues. She also smelled sweaty and it hit me she had been awake all night and had sprayed on more perfume. She started shaking, like in sobs. "Chabney, the river flooded. I thought you were on your way to the ocean."

I had a sense what she was doing was what mothers did to kids escaped from trouble. She must have seen mothers gushing this way on television like everyone had. But she didn't seem one minute older than me anymore, something about her was fourteen. I'd probably turned fourteen since I'd last seen her, as Dad thinks I was born sometime in April, or so his junk certificate had told my school, and April was long gone.

"Man, you're warm," she said. I noticed then those shakes weren't sobs because her voice was clear. She was shivering. "Or I should say, Boy, you're warm."

"Girl, you're chilly." There was something very good about the feel of chilly skin.

"You think I'm a girl? Girls don't work at the church. You know I'm the youngest there by about thirty years? They aren't even women anymore. They're tree trunks." Then she had only her hands on my shoulders and gasped, like she'd caught herself from tripping. "So where do you want these letters?"

"Just give them to me."

Then she was clomping down my stairs again, toward the light spilling out the door. This time I had even less stuff than last and didn't want her to see everything gone. I slammed the deadbolt and followed.

"Man, you put your bed away. But you still got that pile of lightbulbs." She welcomed herself through my door. "Will you get a chair next time for me to sit, if you're gonna keep sending me letters?"

I was hungry. I had also left behind in this basement a beat-up pan with soaked beans, but they had grown plants and other gray things and last night I'd thrown them to the rain. I needed to buy stuff, cut my cell service and save bucks and rethink everything after that grand larceny yesterday, but had no idea if I was staying with the pellet holes or going.

She unstrapped her purse, took out the letters and dropped them next the pan on the counter. On second thought, she added the purse. She brushed her upper arms. "It's so chilly down here, how can you stand it? Where's your coat?"

She had to be asking for my coat for herself, and I felt guilty mine was gone. "It got chilly again only last night." Luckily she forgot her request and stopped nosing. The twenty-four hours had had too many details for me to fuss about. The only luck was she was here and the only bad luck she was in this basement. She opened her arms to get warmed up again. "How come you're so warm?"

"There's a lot of me. You're the one without a coat." I wanted to say, finally had to say, just the one word, "Gawene."

"That's because, last night, just like you said, at first it wasn't cold."

Somehow, in a little while we were sitting on the carpet, still holding on. It was more awkward this way, my nose in her hair that was bushing everywhere. The carpet was cold on the legs and getting dank again with all these rains. I felt bad I had lost my blanket and she would ask for it any minute, but I could not bother her about last night's mess-ups in the rain. And that way, our heads together and looking opposite ways, we started talking. I asked if she'd meant to say she'd been out all last night. No, but she'd been up, hearing the news on the radio, about eleven when the Trinity started rising after six hours' downpours across North Texas. She'd been walking about the house, thinking of me and if I could swim. She'd heard weeks ago at work, through someone who knew someone and so on, about a fellow who sounded like me from the description, staying at the river. Just idle babble. But Tim wouldn't let her go out. Nine years older than her, so he acts like he's her father. I felt terrible because I had been dead asleep by that time, not thinking of her at all. Then Tim conked out when the boubou wore off, and the rain slackened in minutes and she ran out. She came here, though a half dozen times the last couple months she'd seen the place dead. Then she spun around the neighborhood looking at the torn branches and fallen trees, passed back by here a few times like she couldn't believe the silence but didn't knock. And then, she knocked, and here I was. She held me tighter a second and said again, "You're here."

So yeah, she and her brother had stayed on at the house these months and the skeeger and his nasty notes had stayed away. Palla kept on at their mom's in Waxahachie because of the kid though she was about to kick the mom out for undercharging on guns. Now I was looking at Gawene Stevens,

City Limit

Gawene I meant, inches from my nose, and she did look fourteen now. It was because the aquamarine, the purple, all the colors, except her golden brown, were gone. Maybe she looked less Egyptian without the colors, but her cheekbones were still the knobby soft of mushrooms. Her eyes slanted up in a curve at their ends and so did her smile, which you thought was sly. But that firm jaw turned her smile into determined and friendly. She asked what about me, her days were all the same, but I was the one out on my feet. I told her those pellet holes had put me outside a while, that was all.

Then, there's a side of her that's not fourteen, we were kissing. It must have been her who started, our foreheads were so close. We were freezing, her skirt was still wet in places, at the waist, on the panties' elastic. I touched them only a second. I was still dank, too, hadn't noticed until exposed to air. She was the guide, I was the mirror, till she got ticked. "You don't have to do everything I do. I'm the girl, we're a little different." But she had her hand on my chest, and it was the best excuse to put my hand on that round white, that was now behind many open buttons. We both gasped, and I watched my hand move on human silk.

"I like fourteen," she said, "because it's all good."

I was astonished, how much black she had, there where her lines crossed in an X, as much as on the top of her head it seemed. When she reached around and freed more of herself, I watched so long, her eyes went sleepy. But then her hands met behind my neck and I stopped staring.

After a while, I did know enough, we could have a kid, and that made me stupidly happy. Or maybe I could work in the church with her and the tree trunks. She seemed happy, lying back with her chin pushed up and that smile with the ends of the lips curled and her eyes shut. I wondered two seconds if she had felt as wonderful as I had. She had to, everyone carried on so, and just the warm way she felt against me and our hands grabbing everywhere. And she looked so peaceful now, maybe I looked that way too. Long as she dozed, I watched.

Her breasts grew each time she breathed. And when she breathed out, they didn't shrink, they just stayed, and with the next breath they grew again. They kept growing and swelling. At their center the circle was so much darker than the rest of her, how could it be the same skin? Was that skin even, or something more special? And at the center of that circle the smaller circle burst upward and still another kind of skin. It had huge small holes, dozens of them, I imagined tiny open mouths. I had seen breasts before, one at a time out of a dress on a sofa for baby head, all you saw was the curve, but these were different. You had the two outer circles, the two inner ones and then the dot in the middle, like a target. Maybe here's where somebody got the idea for bullseye. You plug for home. Or maybe it's the other way around: The target shape gets the baby's mouth to home in, because mama is too often scattered elsewhere to fit the mouth where it belongs. That's how everyone can't get over breasts.

So I daydreamed. I'd never imagined how a body could get you daydreaming. So that's why you wanted to get that fabric out of the way, so you could wonder. And under all that, somewhere in that skin, was Gawene. And Gawene was all of that too, from the green sparkly painted toes to those stray hairs in the light beam. You clip off some of that green toenail, you clip off some of Gawene. I said it, "Gawene," several times. "Gawene. Gawene."

But she kept sleeping.

She stirred at some time, and stirred me from sleep, too. She showed her watch, and it showed noon. "Got to be at work at one."

She reached around for those same pieces she'd freed herself of long ago. Couldn't she call work and stay the rest of the day, rest of the week? She could not cut herself off from this place all at once. But I let her go right ahead, one of the most horrific sights I'd seen, worse than the bodies I'd seen taken out on litters at Illinois, bodies you don't know. This one I did know, and the worst sight was her packing it up to take away.

"Don't look at me like that," she said. "Tim's not mowing enough lawns for all the dust he needs. And Palla's not doing nothing down in Waxahachie."

She stood, and I did, and she gave up and hugged me. "Was this your first time?"

Of course she could tell, I was so obvious, staring at her and blabbing I'd never thought it'd feel so fine. Maybe I had meant she was what was fine. "No."

"I'm the one oughtta be giving you the looks. I'm the one always here, you're the one never there."

Then she pulled away and strutted to the stairs, and she was twenty again.

22.

That afternoon kept me in the basement, and I was starving. Me and my belly were shrinking. But no knocks, and no shots. Door slams somewhere outside got me as far as the stairwell, till I realized and slumped back.

Night came, I counted the last change the kids had missed from my front pocket, and I bought burgers that vaporized. I slept, sort of, in the doghouse. Next day, I squeezed my bank for the first time ever, as little as I could, and slunk around town hollower in the chest than ever. Hollow because of my monetary future. New pack, change of clothes, new cell. Cut old cell. Like everything, cell bills I paid cash, at the phone store.

Had to get an apartment, soon. Would Gawene give up Tim and Palla?

With new used blankets I lay out on a dry ledge halfway up the levy, river side. I tried to tally clouds, thin baby ones in a hot blue over downtown. But they shifted too much. The river was down almost to its banks but shooting fast as rats. I timed floating boxes, from the Thornton bridge to the Corinth, by going one-thousand-one, one-thousand-two, and did the math to get their speed. 16.3 mph. That kept me till night.

Nights I had to force my body down on the soggy riverbottoms and not let it roam to her house. If she looked out a window and saw me peeking, imagine how that would look, the whites of my eyes in the dark.

Days I was back on my rounds, that cough of a while ago was back, too, bad as that Doberman on the hill under full moon. The routine kept my feet from going where they shouldn't. I kept thinking, If those cops hadn't stopped me, the kids wouldn't have gotten me, I wouldn't have stayed at the basement, I wouldn't have been found by Gawene Stevens, I wouldn't be without her now, I would have drowned. I couldn't add up my luck.

One evening, going down Corinth to Dad's, I did pass near her house. At Morrell I stared up the hill. From there you can't see her house on Moore, but I was sure a few of those treetops were hers.

The visit to the parking lot across from home was my second. Dad never showed. His car was under the orange street light. It was Thursday night, so if he went anywhere, he wouldn't start so late. I stayed till midnight anyway, just in case. But around here the cops could let a car sit for weeks before putting on the red tow-away warning sticker. To walk away from that '78 Honda, I had to push myself.

Time came around for the next bank letter and an excuse to stand on my favorite porch. But all the Stevenses' curtains were shut. It was six o'clock in the afternoon, lots of hot sun, so steamy in front of her door you had to open your collar buttons to breathe. Finally the door creaked to a crack, letting out a huff of stuffy dark air. "Chabney? She ain't home."

It was Palla's voice, more crackly than my cough. It sent me flutters: How did she know who I'd come for? I tried, "Well you're home. That's good as anyone."

"She won't be back for a while."

Me on the city roads all day, could the whole world see into my head? But I needed to find out what "for a while" meant. Or was Gawene hiding inside? I tried, "It's so dark in there. And you got these great windows we don't have in the basement."

"It's too damn hot." Only about every other half-word came out between the voice creaks. "——'Stoo'd ——m'hot."

Then the door shut. She joking? I said too loud, "I didn't come just for her."

No one opened up. Not a snap of the floor boards. What if Palla tells Gawene I had not come for Gawene? Palla should not know a thing about me and Gawene. What if Gawene had heard me just now, saying I hadn't come only for her?

Evenings past dusk I allowed myself to pass her house. Blinds and curtains stayed shut, but light shined through their edges. Sometimes a blind was open, one in the back, you could tell by the light on the bushes. Gawene's room was in back. The Stevenses had no fence. I dared a run through the backyard. It was an actual run since I was still losing me and my belly. The blind was open all right, but no Gawene.

A few different nights when the bushes were glowing, I dared but found nothing except once Tim Stevens stooped at her bed peeking under. I was getting scared I would have to go by her church office and not like what I heard.

It was deep summer, katydids howling so loud in the trees I couldn't hear my own feet, and I spotted her in her room. So happy she was alive I almost sped right on. But her stillness caught me. Standing, she was looking up, lips parted. At first I thought she was praying, learned something at work. But her eyes were drifting. Then her hand shot in the air, shut, and opened in a starburst, and she looked disappointed. How would I get her attention without making her squawk? Then, like she felt someone watching, she broke out of trance and went for the blinds. I blurted, "Gawene, it's me." I always blurt.

Her brother and sister could have heard me, but she smushed her face against the panes. I'd come only feet from the window.

In five seconds she was easing the back door shut behind her. But she stopped at arm's length. "Didn't I tell you don't keep disappearing?" She handed me the letters, two more already. "You're one cruel man. Boy."

I told about Palla, and the dark house in the bright day, I'd been trying, really trying. Palla hadn't told her a thing, it turned out. "But that's how Palla's been, all right, since she's been back, keeping that baby in the dark, her highbeam eyes can't stand the light. Okay, it sounds like you tried."

She really stood apart. No big hugging thanks I was alive now the rains had gone. She kept looking behind at the house. "What's with the nerves?" I said. "Palla seemed to know why I dropped by."

"I don't tell Palla everything, but she's not stupid. I just can't let her know too much because she talks." So their mom in Waxahachie had thrown Palla out for stinking the house with yimyom smoke. Their mom held onto the baby a while, to keep its eyes out of the mist. But Palla hovered around and, while her mom hung laundry, stole the baby from off the porch. Now, here on Moore, the skeeger and his threats stayed away the past few months, so Tim felt safe enough. Only problem Gawene had with the house these days was the mosquitoes from the rains. She'd been swatting them tonight when I'd appeared. And, well, there was Palla at the house, too.

Palla blabbed at everyone who dropped by, specially when the patico swam in her veins. She liked to harp how Gawene strutted through the house like the Bride of Frankenstein every time the lightning bolts hit. "There she goes, squeaking at the joints cause her little fourteen-year-old piper ass is out getting wet," Palla said for everyone.

"I don't go squeaking like that," Gawene told me. "Just that one time it flooded and Tim wouldn't let me out and finally I went and found you. And Tim had to go blow it to Palla because they're the piedras twins. And her raspberry ass can't stand it I'd worry about anyone but her."

Palla called her sister "piper's bait," everyone laughed but everyone talked and Gawene's workplace was only a mile away. So Gawene gave me this four foot gap tonight, and I felt bad for all the eyes at windows that might have watched me stalking.

So I told her I'm getting a car, it'll be my place. I didn't have the guts to add it'll be our place but I said I could take her anywhere too and an apartment was my next step. Husker Metcalf and other trusty people I bought from were too honest and law-abiding to sell a car to a fourteen-year-old and watch him drive it off the lot, if they'd had one to sell. So I was dropping by this evening for any noise she might have heard about cars.

"You think if I know a car, I'd break the law and get it for you?" This evening she was more than twenty.

But a notice had hung on the church office bulletin board a couple weeks, for a '94 Nissan Sentra for only $800. It was one of the tree trunks', and they were so stumpy and basic that the car had to be good. Gawene had seen it, a green thing, and for that price, it looked new. No one had bitten yet, everyone already had a car, but Gawene had put in first dibs. She could certainly use a car so summer days she wouldn't arrive at work smelling like nine innings of baseball. "Only I don't have the cash," she said. "I pay the rent." Tim's lawn take went for groceries, I gathered, that is hamburger helper, cakes, sugar block. She feared the car at that price would disappear any day.

"What if I bought," I said, "and when you get enough cash, I'll sell it to you and get me another from someone who doesn't mind breaking law to sell it to me."

"Who ever said anyone ever minded selling it to you? Maybe it could be a present, if someone got me a present of $800."

23.

It took a week, first to wait out the weekend to Monday, tap the piggy bank, cash the check, then to get the cash to Gawene, talk her into putting the title in my name as a "gift." But finally I was gripping the wheel of my green thing. It left me about $400 in savings, to whip my business back into form.

She wouldn't get in the passenger seat beside me. We were in the Wynnewood shopping center parking lot, the dropoff point, so she had a long hot walk home ahead. I assured her that, me driving very illegal without insurance, I'd drive even safer. I'd driven with Dad plenty enough, when he was too bouboued for the wheel. She kept standing. I said, "Don't tell me I bought this car for you and you won't ride in it."

"You bought it for business."

"I bought it because you were fussing about my safety, and you say I'm still not safe enough."

It took another week, but she climbed in. Right out front of her house.

She smelled the new Chabney. Every night I was sleeping in a new neighborhood, fine neighborhoods, Kessler Park, Arcadia Park, Mountain Creek Lake. You just drive into these winding streets of spotlighted brick homes, park, leap into the back seat, maybe a little cramped, curl into your hands and steal the dreams of tycoons. I wanted to get out even further, say Cedar Hill, if I could overcome my fears and break out of the city. Mornings I pull my five-gallon tub to a public sink in a park, or a spigot under some cedar trees, and while I sponge up, for once I care that the birds are carousing. Hair washed every day, two changes of clothes in the trunk and laundry twice a week, no surprise I sell four pieces in four days. You come out of shined car with combed hair and button-down shirt, they're already taking out their wallets for your presentation package alone.

Or my new Forzieris were doing the work.

Standing on her porch she sniffed the peach shampoo in my hair. "You scrubbed the river off you," she said.

And when I opened the passenger door, I told her sniff there too. I'd scrubbed out that morning-after odor of used cars' carpets and buffed the plastic dashboard and armrests. She still kept to her feet. "What if they do pull you over and see my name was on the title and I gave it to you, and I'm the guilty party sitting right there."

"It ain't wrong to give somebody a car. They only care about who's driving."

She looked at me, raising her cheek, like she would ask to see my lawyer's license. She's the one they could brush the chemical dust out of her pores, and she's worried who's legal. "You did make it a whole week without scratching the paint," she said. She bent for another sniff. "And it is fresh inside."

And she sat.

I drove her downtown. Friday evening, and the skyscraper streets were empty except for the tram and its bell. We wound around to the West End and its old brick warehouses and brick streets near the Book Depository, where Dad once had clients. She was in her work clothes, loose skirt past the knees and tight blouse without buttons in their open slits. She said she felt too grungy from working in the air conditioner all day in these threads to go into Spaghetti Warehouse. But hunger pushed her, and we each had a pile with mushrooms and meatballs. When the sun fell and left some purple, I escorted her up the road to Turtle Creek. The air under all those willow trees flopping over the creek was blue green and heavy enough to swim through. Way behind a hundred branches, spotlights were hitting somebody's granite walls. I pointed out the streets where I planned to sleep one night, there at the place with the five arches on the porch, or that one with twenty tall white columns, or the yellow stucco one with the statues from, I swear, the Nile River.

Then I swung her back home, my home. She had never seen Illinois, or Dad, since that Sunday I'd left him. We could watch for Dad awhile. I had stopped by only one night that week, quick, since I'd had a nine o'clock appointment down past Fruitdale Park.

We parked in the store lot, and she gave my old grounds a better gape than she had my favorite Highland Park villa. "That one afternoon I came here, I never thought about it, but now that I see it, I see why you liked High Hat so much."

"I knew High Hat, that was all."

Dad's car was gone. She started yawning because, I gathered, she'd missed her bobo tonight. When I'd picked her up Tim hadn't returned from work and interplanetary mission. Though she tried to tell me she didn't do bobo no mo. She said, "You can't just come out here and watch your Dad come and go like he's a buffalo at the Marsalis Zoo. He's your Dad. Why don't you go talk to him?"

When I had to scoot her back home to her powder puff, his car was still gone.

She said don't call at work, don't call Tim's cell. So I had to track her down on Moore Street.

Into fall we sat out on the cedar hills over Mountain Creek Lake while the sun put yellow slant across the water. It was dropping sooner and sooner, the yellow going deep and orange. The softie car had killed my walking and returned a lot of softie me to myself, and she liked laying her head on my belly and jabbering. She had a lot of statistics on the neighborhood which she picked up at work, or from Tim's and Palla's hand-to-hand men, or neighbors, or her morning walks. Gawene's friendly; how else had she got to know me. She told of people blown away, all over Oak Cliff. She said even more people got blown away when those airplanes hit those skyscrapers up North, as if she had to mention it when everybody was talking about it. Heck, those planes boosted my sales. I did go sleepy with her tales.

One hot night, we were sitting on a bench above the lake, leaning into each other, she mentioned a girl down on the alphabet avenues who blasted out her little brother. I didn't think about it much, another stat, then she talked about how the kid wore Catwoman getup and then caught her kid brother putting some of it on himself.

I sat up. "How old was she?

"They say about thirteen or fourteen. But looked ten."

"You hear what kind of gun?" I remember most of my customers and what I got them, I don't know why unless, in case they see me in the streets again, I know what kind of barrel might poke at me from a jacket.

Gawene batted her eyelids. I was scaring her, so interested in her story about guns. She rarely told the gun details, unless it had been a surprise sawed-off attack or derringer from a purse. Shaking her head she said, like I was forcing the words out of her, "I don't know. They said the freak thing was, it was some kind of high-powered rifle. Up close, it went right through the boy's brain."

I got up to my feet and was walking. Or maybe running. A deer rifle. Remington. I'd bought it off the lumberyard fence with a couple other pieces right after I'd opened the bank account. Been unable to sell them, thought a wino in my basement had jinxed me, so here came this girl on the sidewalk. With a red Catwoman purse.

Gawene was clomping heels after me on the hard dirt, but I couldn't let her see my face. Of course guns shoot, and the ones Dad and I sold could shoot, and one I'd sold damn near shot me. But it hadn't killed me. And I'd heard shots all times of day and seen a blasted body or two pulled out at Illinois. But never were our customers on those litters. And I'd hear of people shipping out to Laurel Land, but those had to have been Rick Ocotillo's jobs.

Even in her heels she caught up with my damn fat legs. I bunched my head in my arms so she couldn't see. I don't know how long since I'd cried, but I seemed to make up for time. Stupid, all I cared about was that skinny girl without breasts, saw her holding that deer rifle at her brother. That skinny girl watching her brother's blood hit the walls. I didn't even care about the brother, just her and her Catwoman getup, dropping the rifle and staring.

Gawene was fallen over me, and I'd fallen on the grass, and I told her I'd be okay, it was just a shock, I didn't like to hear about kids getting blown away.

"I'm sorry," she said. "I had told you about other kids. I had told you cause it got to me. I thought—in your business, I didn't know how much it got to you."

"It was the deer rifle. That's too much."

"You don't think you knew them, do you?"

I shook my head and rose to my ass and swiped a backhand over my face.

She tried to place her arms around me like I knew she'd seen mothers do on television shows, so I got up and walked to the car.

24.

Business was working me hard. Only I tried not to sell to kids anymore, anyone under fourteen. It was not hard to since with car and cell I worked mostly by leads and appointments, like Dad. After buying the car I'd sold to only a couple kids anyway.

Calls were taking me out wider and wider, almost to Grand Prairie and Balch Springs and Red Bird Airport, and crannies of Oak Cliff I'd never thought about, like the oily swamps by Lemon Lake or white cliffs above Clarendon where a band of guys had huts in the woods. But business still centered me in the heavy chemicals around South Ervay, guys in the peeling wood base houses across from the tool shops.

I had my favorite spots to do repairs. Kiest Park is wide and rolling with clumps of cedar trees, and in the middle of it I can breathe. There you have a covered slab of picnic tables that's boiling with families weekends but weekday mornings is quiet as folded hands. You can view the park roads a quarter mile around, and cops or bone heads rarely crawl through that time of morning. I like how the park roads snake through, and on both sides they have a knee-high log post every ten or twenty feet. The sight makes me feel I'm not in the city but in some other neck of history

Nights I made it to Dad's every couple weeks, to sit in the lot and watch for him. All my life I thought I knew his schedule. But all I knew was blobs of time in his schedule, when he might come or go. I had to watch for him because he needed watching, he could not do too well on his own. Even in this car that he couldn't know, I began at dark and parked in a shadow. I also didn't want to attract Rick Ocotillo's eye. I parked my own eye on Dad's shut front door or his Honda's empty space. I promised myself that when he appeared this time I'd run out and say hello, like Gawene had told me to. But when that parking space did fill with a car or the door in the boards jiggled open, I stuck to my seat. He shuffled along, craggy, bent, slow for a bone head. Sometimes he stopped and talked to someone. I got a strong happy relief each time he showed up alive, and then, I couldn't say why, my door stayed shut. Rick Ocotillo, I told myself. When Dad shut his front door behind him or drove off, I drove on, telling myself that once I had my own place, something to give him for leaving him, I would run out and get him, Rick Ocotillo or not.

Dark coming colder and closer on six o'clock, Gawene and I lost Mountain Creek Lake. We just drove the night-time streets or sometimes dropped cash into spaghetti or burgers at a table. She talked more about herself, trimmed the body counts. She told how she'd grown up in Waxahachie and how hers and Tim's Daddy had sold antiques, really just rusty crud from old barns outside town. Then he died, they said, when a loading crane bonked him on a weekend job he'd taken since the antiques didn't pay.

Her mom the white lady took over the antiques, did well at it at flea markets, started hawking anything, paintings, potted plants, bullets, even once an old cannon. When Gawene was a kid she played for years in the empty mixer of a cement truck, until her Mom sold it and the kids screamed. Gawene had about nine or ten brothers and sisters, she wasn't sure, many from her dad's earlier marriage since his wife died. The older ones left.

Tim, her oldest real brother, left twelve years ago, at seventeen, came to Dallas on a lead from a customer of their mom's, at the gravel yard. The gravel dust gave him asthma, he quit, but a few years later when he started mowing lawns dust stopped bothering him. Palla came up to have her first kid and escape her mom, but lost the kid before it was born. Gawene was the only to finish school, visited Tim weekends and stopped by the church nearby for services because she liked the name, "Cliff Temple." She liked how the sunlight broke in from high up, down through the stained glass. She thought it was what the man meant when he talked about the light. A bulletin board note there got her a job typing in the church office, summer after she graduated.

We were in the back seat by now, under the blanket in the cold. Her skin pressed against me, and I was getting scared my own breasts were starting to size up like hers. Her tales made me drowsy as tales and skin should. For a while she asked me to talk about myself as well, till she saw I was right--I didn't have any more to me than what happened in a business day, so many buys and sales. We went quiet a while, and she said my name over and over. "Chabney. Chabney." I tried saying her name over and over, "Gawene. Gawene," but gave up as I sounded like a bad echo.

One night she was getting drowsy against me as well, and mumbled so I could barely hear, "Chabney. Chabney, name like that, your mom had to have black in her." I don't have much to say about who came from who. I figured she was teasing, but after a while she went on. "I never said, but I think I saw who your mom might a been." Gawene had to know I didn't talk about who came from who, but she went on. "Back when I first came here visiting Tim in Dallas, eight-nine years ago.

117

This man Arn said he had a kid, and whenever he came by, you were in school, even weekends. He'd visit Tim more back then, Tim said, couple times a month, some weekends when I visited. He came once with a woman, he was real nervous and quiet that time, bought a lot off us, I thought he was paying her off something." Gawene got nervous and quiet herself, trembling, I couldn't tell why. "She was too dark for a white lady, I figured part black or Indian. I always thought I could tell black, but I couldn't this time. Then when I first saw you, first thing came to mind was that woman. She was big, like you. I always wondered, Arn's such a twig."

"I ain't big, I'm chubby." I held back about Dad's former potbelly.

"And the same color. But it's the nose, you have this small nose but it's beaked at the top like an Indian's. She had it. But I told myself it was black anyway, name like Chabney, different, original you know but almost like another name. Like Gawene is. My black daddy named me, not my white mom. I wanted to tell you about that woman, long time. Tim once said how your Dad had let slip one day, how he'd gone to Arizona to get you after you were born, from your grandma. When I saw this woman with Arn, I thought it must have been her he'd taken you from. Arn ever tell you if she's Indian or got some black, or other stuff about her?"

Gawene had to know I wasn't interested in what Gawene was saying, for once, and her skin started feeling heavy. I turned aside to breathe some of the cool air out the blanket. I said, "How come you think Dad don't come by no mo?"

"He don't talk about her, right?"

"I guess we don't."

"Don't you want to know you're from black or Indian?" She was trying to put out that comfort hand she'd seen on television.

It was time to free a passenger and go scout a place to sleep, tomorrow had work. I pulled some clothes off the floor. "I'm hitting fifteen just fine as it is."

"You don't even go walk up to your Dad who loves you. No wonder he don't visit us no more. He knows you might drive up."

"He's the one don't ask where I am."

"And you don't even ask where your mom is, your own mom you lived inside."

"No one's turning down anyone's visits."

I don't know how we got on this topic, but I got dressed and started driving while she dressed in back. When she was done, I stopped and let her in front. I was happy we stayed quiet a few miles. I don't know why I had to say one last thing, but I did. "I've seen magazine photos, Indians out west, maybe Arizona even, saw that kind of beak at the top, like mine. Yeah, so that was mine, I figured, freaky to see it in a magazine. But I also seen pictures of lizards' paws, know how much they look like a person's hand? And I seen horses' knees, lot like mine when I've been walking too much. And chimpanzee's eyes. And the palms of their hands, the palms of their hands. They got hands. Like us."

All I knew was, she was the one with boubou in the blood, and boubou makes you blubber unimportant stuff, like Dad and his voices of the gods. But she had the life worth telling, and our nights out she learned to stick to hers and stayed off mine.

25.

In the winter her mom passed. She asked me to the funeral, at a white cardboard box of a church down near Lancaster with clear smeary windows. I kept expecting Dad to walk in. Only about twenty folks came, and their footsteps and whispers echoed on the bare walls. It was the only time with her family that I was so aware who was the roundest, maybe because I was the only one she cried into. So about twenty knew about us if they hadn't before.

For weeks she stared into nowhere, and her face seemed to drop an inch down her skull. But she talked about anyone else but her mom and held onto me longer and harder than ever, so hard I had to free my neck for air. She said her brothers' and sisters' necks were too skinny to fall on.

About on time for my fifteenth birthday, which was possibly in April, she told me, "You can see this as a birthday present, but I don't know how much you're going to want it. But I don't care if you don't." It was a Sunday, we were in Lake Cliff Park, where they have white and purple irises in big green clumps around the shore. It was right in that time between cool and warm you get in spring, when the grass is soaked just a half-inch under your ass but the sun's knifing through the clouds. "I did a home pregnancy test, and you've been my only this last year, Chabney. It's yours, and maybe you'll want it."

It took me some seconds just to crack open her words, she was so roundabout. "You saying you got a baby coming, and I'm the daddy?"

"I didn't think you'd be terrified. Maybe not care a hoot. But look at your eyes."

"I ain't terrified. I just couldn't tell what you're getting at." I was also taking some seconds to believe I of all people, after sleeping by rivers and walking too much, could have one of those squealing creatures in my hands.

She cupped a hand on her mouth. "Lord, you're only fifteen, Chabney. I knew it but I don't know why I never thought about it. You're too young to be anybody's daddy, you can't even drive with a license."

"Of course I want the kid. I know people who are thirty and shouldn't drive with a license. We'll get an apartment. I've saved enough for plenty months' rent."

But she kept biting her lips and shaking her head. "Man I don't think about things. I mean boy I don't. I'm going on twenty-two, and you can't even buy cigarettes. Man have I been living on another planet."

She didn't snap out of her new weird attitude for weeks. I read in a women's magazine a woman can get scared when she's pregnant, her body's roasting chemicals strong as hamburger helper. I did get her to promise to get off the hamburger helper, which I'd read could roast the growing baby. But then she accused me, "You didn't even have a mother around to help you as a kid, how can you help one with a kid? You don't even care who your mother is, how can you care who I am?"

And Tim and Palla were back in her news. We go months without a ripple from them, then after their mom's death they're capsizing. "They don't have your green Sentra to get away in," she said. Tim found another real skeeger among his hand-to-hand men. This one liked to pound his fist against Tim's wall like a judge's mallet, with his thumb sticking out. He told the whole room he was rhino man and he'd bunt out anyone who bought elsewhere. Tim chided the guy on, and they had a shouting contest at two A.M. She had never seen Tim so noisy and rash. "He wasn't that close to Mom, but something's chiseled his head," Gawene said. Then turns out Palla's carrying on with the skeeger, probably just to get Tim back for kissing Mom off and bringing on her end. And now Palla, Gawene swore, was pregnant from this skeeger, who was moving in next door and threatening Tim insisting he move out and free up his house for him and Palla, and threatening neighbors, screaming at them at midnight. And Gawene came home too many afternoons to find the baby, the one already born, dried in the mouth and rolling on the bathroom floor.

And one neighbor, Gawene told me in July, walked right into that room the skeeger rented next door, Saturday 10:35 A.M., and scattered his parts. Sawed-off, point blank. She'd been with me that morning; we'd gone to look at a new used car so our kid wouldn't have to ride with gun oil. Tim didn't tell her for days, and neither did the neighbors, but Palla had disappeared so he explained. It had been a man right down on Lynnhaven. Neighbors knew, but they feared him and hated the noisy skeeger too much to rat.

The sawed-off and Lynnhaven started working into me gradual as a screw. I asked if she knew the man. She did, so I said describe. He was big, had a mustache, maybe Mexican or Indian.

I said, "He had a dog house. He let me stay in his dog house." But that was all I told her. We needed a way to buy that other car.

For months I was falling back too much on a supplier off Industrial, in the warehouses. I didn't like warehouses, they were too obvious and you saw a lot more Dallas black-and-whites snooping those streets. I liked joints like Husker Metcalf's and the old man behind the transmission shop, but I'd sucked those joints to bone, and still I went back to skim them every couple months. This guy off Industrial, the yellow warehouses on all four sides were empty, gates chained, loading docks cracking. You had to get to him by creeping down an alley. You rapped a code, $- - - \cdot - - \cdot - -$, a video camera watched you, he answered with an intercom. He slid the door up, wearing baggy black karate pants, a green scarf tied on an ankle, no shirt, showing the abs of a double grid of Hostess Twinkies. I doubt he paid rent. He wasn't too old, nineteen or twenty, looked white as piano keys but talked everything from black to beige. I used him because he always had plenty of shiny gage that wanted little tooling.

Over summer I was looking for a spot for Gawene and the new one and pictured opening a store myself, say on West Jefferson, opposite end of Jefferson from Harran's. Maybe I could buy from Industrial Man here for my first inventory, then go to legit warehousers. So when I stopped by in July I must have had piper smeared all over my face, like I'd bow over and tie his green ankle scarf. I was buying a record seven gages, and he squinted hard like he was finally giving me a first good look. "You my mark, dude," he said. "It's time you be down with me, you know, we gonna court you in. I'm king, and I need someone holding down your hood."

He was laying the talk on so heavy and unnatural, he had to be joking. "Joe King," I said. "Who says I'm in any hood."

"I know where you is. One of them boys you sell to needs checking in, maybe take him outta the box. I need a road dog holding down there. You always strapped, you just the one to run a mission, pull off some red rum."

I didn't give his blabber much. He struck me as a lot of breath like too many salesmen. When I sell, I just say what I got and move on. Once or twice, customers ribbed me about courting me into their cliques. But it was all fun on both sides. The man they're buying gage from, they don't usually even joke, or don't too far. Because as I say, they think their man can shoot, and they don't know me and my lack of plug time.

Then he said, "Don't say you ain't in any hood, you and your ruby red up on Morrell all a time."

For the first time at a supplier's, I got a case of shakes. I had never driven Gawene anywhere near Industrial. This guy had somebody's eyes on me. Maybe only his own two. Maybe he only once glanced at Gawene and me near Morrell. I wanted to leave without making the purchase. But if I took a step he might see my shakes.

I waited for them to go, but he was waiting for an answer. My shoulders and chest started vibrating so, you could see it right through my tight button-down, I'd put on so much weight. I had no answer except no. Not a good answer. I was waiting for a better one, much as he was. My head was empty and cold as that dog house. Then a better answer barged in. "I know the man for you," I said. "Best shot in Dallas."

"I thought you the best shot."

My hand dug in my pocket for the pay. A bad move, because he jerked. The gages were in a box on a two-wheeler. I opened and dropped the wad on the floor and pushed the two-wheeler. "Seven hundred. My man'll call you."

I got the two-wheeler to dock's edge, leapt off and opened my trunk, expecting my head to flash in orange light. But I made it to my ignition, I believe because for once I had to stick around on Earth, for the new one on its way.

A week later I brushed past Dad. I was buying parts at Harran's, and old boy Harran was adding up the purchases in his blind rat way. He didn't look up when behind me the door opened and feet wandered to a counter across the room. I didn't look around, either, not till I got to the door, and maybe curiosity made me turn, because I never see other customers there. I fear the old guy will go broke. Or maybe I recognized those sliding footsteps. But leaning at a counter was Dad, back to me. There's only so many customers and alleys in our Oak Cliff. Still, showing up not thirty feet away, he shocked me.

First thing I noticed, his shirt tail was out. His presentation package never allowed such a hang. It blew out so loose while he bent, his bones looked closer to the surface than ever. His shoulder blades sent up a couple of V's. Harran was still crabbing over his cash box and didn't see us. "Be with you in a minute," he hollered at the new customer. I was about to run up and fall at Dad's boots. There was my "best shot in Dallas," even if crack left him far from a crack shot, and of course I'd hardly meant calling him to the Industrial Man. But then—when Dad had stumbled into the store, he had to have noticed me. No one my age but me wears Forzieris.

And he had to hear the traffic through the open door. Deaf Harran did, glanced up but returned to his crabbing. Was Dad so stooped and roasted he couldn't hear, had forgotten the outline of my body? Maybe to him I was no more here in Harran's than I'd ever been in his basement.

I must have watched a minute at that door, and both old boys stayed crabbed at their counter.

26.

In August Gawene placed my hand on her stomach and this time I felt something. Maybe all I felt was the results of her race to catch up with me. She must have added an inch to the upper arms and chin, two inches to the legs, three to the chest, and her hair had spiked four more inches since spring. But now I had her stand tall and upright beside the picnic table in her tight orange dress, and now you could imagine something more than all that extra spaghetti, something more like a small head starting to round out.

Feeling that hint of a bulge, I told myself before I told her aloud, I was putting down money tomorrow on one of three chances I had for digs.

"Doctor told me it's real all right but I can keep working," she said, like she had to quiet my thought she was merely eating too much. "My one big hangup is doctors. Before this visit I hadn't been to one since, oh, a polio booster back in Waxahachie."

"I'm coming with you next time."

"You don't have to. And then you thinking I'm starting to show, don't you. Imagine the women at the office. Either I wear baggy dresses like I never and then they know, or regular ones like this and I show, or maternity stuff and then they really know, and I can't afford that maternity anyway, man it's not priced for people that work. I mean boy. I mean man. Show or know, whatever way, I got about a month, and they'll start seeing who's not married. And I can't lose this job."

Somehow the tree trunks already knew about Palla. A couple months after her skeeger went away Palla showed up at home. Now she was showing big, lying on the living room floor while her first love child practiced the marathon in the other rooms. None of the Stevenses told those church women, but the church women knew, probably from poking their noses out the church windows and sniffing neighborhood brush fires. "That sister still at home all day?" they'd ask Gawene. "Too bad your mom ain't there to watch the children."

"Children?" Gawene said to me.

So the neighborhood talked, but her big fear of the gas leak was its traveling down Lynnhurst to the man with the mustache. She didn't want him coming in the house to clean up traces of Skeeger Junior.

She sat on my lap at the picnic table. I liked that weight. I liked to feel the thighs spread across mine instead of bones. Weight is such good human stuff. Her face up close in the daylight had twice as much cheek. The aquamarine around the eyes had gone as green as the cedar needles hanging into the picnic shed. A new sweetsour odor poured off her, just made me want to hold her longer.

"You hooked up with me, don't worry about that job," I said.

"I'm not saying hook up with me just because those women see I don't have a ring."

"I'll get you a ring."

"Anyone can get a ring. If they know about Palla already, they'll know what's only a ring."

"So we'll do the papers and go to the chapel."

"At your age? You know you need your daddy's permission? Then what'll people sniff about me in those brush fires? 'She's twenty-two and he's fifteen.'"

She was pushing back, all the way back from me, giving me sideways eyes and chokeholding my neck. I'd thought she was long past this weird phase fretting about who has which birth date. Then she threw herself back at me, with all those fine new pillows of hers. Then she was shaking. It wasn't nerves. "You're older than Tim, and he's already past thirty. I don't know anyone stays hooked up, but I've known you forever, you always been around, I don't think you're going to stop." She was sniffling. "But you have to get your dad's okay, Mr. Lawman, that's the state who asks for the numbers. Finally you gotta go talk to your old man and not just look at him."

"And I gotta go find a birth certificate."

I laid out the plan: Right away I firm up the apartment, get her and our upcoming away from Palla and Tim. She still had a month or two before growing too public, plenty time for me to track down the old man.

One of my customers was an old white woman in a yellow wood house near Kiest Park. She'd bought three times, always double-barreled 16-gauge Winchesters, she said for her nephews to hunt duck. I believed her, not that I needed to, but her dead old man's duck pictures hung under small lamps in the living room. I don't know why she bought from me except for the home delivery and a relative had tipped her off about my prices. Out back she was redoing a big garden shed for living quarters to rent, "I hope to a new couple." Last May I told her give me first dibs, and she said I had it. But here it was August and the stacks of tar shingles were only breaking open their paper wraps from the rainstorms.

I got too impatient and flapped my mouth elsewhere. Another regular I called Rick Junior to myself, maybe five or ten years younger than Rick Ocotillo, say twenty-five. But he seemed an actual landlord, one the law approves, though I don't know if much more legitimate. He owned a row of apartments off Beckley between Kiest and Illinois, another row off Cockrell Hill, and a scatter of shotgun shacks in the alphabet avenues. Every couple months he bought a bag of my cheapest pistols, probably resold to his hooked tenants. We met in one of his recently emptied spaces that always reeked of bleach, or sometimes in his 320ZX that dripped with cheap musk oil. He wore a coat to his knees even in August, threw the bag in an inside pocket, and he was so bony no one would perceive a bulge. His face was narrow as a pistol grip. His only resemblance to Rick Ocotillo was a suit, but blue and with a tie.

I let slip one day I needed a place. In Dallas you can't rent without a rent history, and Gawene didn't have one herself. I asked Rick Junior what he could get me, and he said about anything he had, and he had 186 units. But then, he started leaving voicemail for more than gun orders. "Hot 2-bedroom, eat-in kitchen, balcony, huge bathtub, I got photos, and I'll leave the gunrack up." "Avenue G one-bedroom home, yard, fence, quadruple-locked doors, I'll email photos, first month free, nothing down."

Say I take up his offer, and build my rental history. Then in a year, I try an actual legit landlord, one without nose rings. This landlord will listen to Rick Junior? He'll ask for my work history. So I'd have to go to Rick the Third, then Rick the

Fourth, and they'll ask for my bags of cheapos and I stay in their loop.

When I didn't reply for weeks, he started throwing voicemail fits. "I offer the cream of Oak Cliff, I squeeze this last guy out of his box to free up a home for you and your ruby, you gouge me forever with premium prices for shoddy scrap metal. You think you and ruby red are hiding from me?"

I hate people unloading their air.

Another customer was a preacher at a small Pentecostal church in a former Woolworth's, after the chain shut down. It still had the luncheonette, for Sunday fellowship dinner. His office was the manager's upstairs, with a view window so the manager could watch for shoplifters. The room bubbled with the store's actual old aquariums and their blue inchlong fish. He was a black fellow with red hair and wore dungarees weekdays because for the week he worked his farm plot outside town, vegetables he donated to charity along with, I guessed, the pistols. He said he bought for flock safety. When he told me his old tenant in the farmhouse was moving out September 15, I put the cash on his desk right away.

The place was twenty miles south of town; he didn't even have photos. Gawene would commute, maybe I could hunt ducks.

There were a couple weeks toward the end of summer where I missed her. Our habit was Friday at six I'd pick her up at the Marsalis Zoo entrance, which was halfway between her work and home. But she made a rare call to my cell, voicemail saying she'd be late with preparations for the upcoming Sunday School year.

City Limit

My leg was bouncing in my driver's seat, anxious to go tell her about the house. I went by her room window, like I did nights when we hadn't made plans, but the room was dark, the house quiet. The dark sight sent me the shakes like she'd never given because I could always find her. In weeks we'd have our house and I'd get her a phone. How had we lasted this long by hit or miss?

Saturday, business kept me to almost midnight, and the next week had me chasing one ghost customer after another, appointments who didn't show up. August only heats up my line of trade, and people get notions they want to buy more heat. Nights, I was so ragged I could only manage to hunt for a tree to park under.

Next Friday I waited at Marsalis Zoo, with the shakes so bad even at a quarter to six I was out the car and pacing past the ticket booth. Peacocks back in the trees were griping, and a big cat gnashing so much somewhere behind the foliage I could see it lapping around its cage like me. I was exploding with the house news, I'd waited over a week to tell her. I'd waited so long just to tell her with all the explosion in me.

By seven, I'd eaten two balls of cotton candy and was shaking to the pit of my belly. How had I gone so long not buying her a phone? Her family couldn't afford one more cell, she told me save my money. I'm always caving in, but I should have bought her one anyway. She had always been there, where she was supposed to. I could never think she wouldn't be.

Me and the car crept up Marsalis to Jefferson and the big old church. It was dark as its brown bricks. I sped along the routes she'd told me she'd walked, all the way to her house. It was dark too.

I went back through all the routes and back, slow, fast, till midnight.

Sunday I said to myself, who cares what Tim and Palla say, and I walked onto the front porch. The boards creaked like arguing sparrows. They were dusty. Junkmail was fussing for space in the letter box. I had let Gawene go through it for my bank mail. A pot of flowers looked dried and forgotten near the door. When I knocked I expected Palla's baby to cry, but the knocks only echoed on the street.

Bedtime that night I pointed the car up Morrell to Moore Street to park and sleep out front, but turned to a safer neighborhood. On Moore I would have just stayed watching anyway. Eight in the morning I drove up and parked a little down Moore so I could see both back and front. She had to head out to work sometime. But on the front door was a red poster, and yellow tape slopped around the porch. I'd seen those red signs and yellow tape on doors at Illinois. I hated thinking how long it'd taken the city to get around to slapping it all up this time.

On their own my fingers switched on the ignition, and then I was at the church. I was wearing my Forzieris and a dress shirt, and I was washed and shampooed to see Gawene. Never been inside but knew from all she said you took a left after the front entrance.

I should be used to entering unknown places, but I approached three times and kept on down the sidewalk. My heartbeat seemed to say enough. But I had to hear from a human.

The office was only one story but glass and aluminum, jutting off the back of the big old brick temple. Gawene said

133

they had ripped down scads of their cool old classroom buildings that were like mazes, and full of underground passages. Too many folks were sneaking in, turning those catacombs into base houses, probably one of my old fences himself. They kept surprising early Sunday School teachers turning on the classroom lights to find a roomful of highbeamers sprawled across the floor.

At the front entrance now, a lady behind the thick glass doors buzzes you in and asks your business. I said I needed Gawene Stevens's office, and she gave me bug eyes but I kept walking left before she could say more. She said, "Young man, young man. I'll phone them."

Next you make a right, and there the pool of desks opens, and a couple women standing together over folders in hand looked up at me while the intercom phone beeped. Gawene said she worked in that pool, and I told myself she was on bathroom break. I wanted to keep telling myself that story and turn and walk out front and wait till she came home tonight. But now I was inside and the front desk lady was beeping them and any direction I went I would hear anyway, so I said, "I need to tell Gawene something."

They kept the folder open. From a desk came a throat sound. Other folks in their seats stopped rustling papers. One of the standing women, getting rigid, as if I weren't dressed so well, said all angry, "What do you need to tell her?"

"About a house."

The intercom phone kept beeping. She said, eyes glowing angry, working hard to keep down her voice, "Don't you know?"

"I don't know. What?"

"She passed away. Days ago. Are you here for personal matters?"

I think I ran out of there.

III.

27.

I don't know what I did the rest of that day, or that week. All I know is for two years I pretty much stayed with the car. When it was in the shop, I lay out by the river a couple days until it was ready. I learned basic repairs, starting with my own toolkit. A car is only an oversized weapon, so many screws and bolts, only not so subtle as a handheld version. On very cold nights, I looked for a dry empty basement on High Hat. Rick Ocotillo and his sort stay home when it's too frosty. My cough came back with a whirlwind and dug a den in my lungs.

Once a week I made it my regular schedule to go watch Dad from the strip mall, my best recreation, better than magazines. Because I could sit with my eyes planted on his parking space and on his unit behind and empty my head. It was a game: From one second to the next, I could guess, Would it be the next second he appears? And I'd lay bets with myself, which I kept reworking, adding up points for and against myself. I could do it till I fell asleep. But if I tried reading magazines, I couldn't go ten lines. In a Dallas magazine if someone was beautifying Turtle Creek with irises, I'd see the irises at Lake Cliff Park where she told me about her condition. If I'd read about Panama banana plantations and they talked about how they had tenant farmers, then I saw that preacher's farmhouse I never saw. An article about Roger Moore and I saw her street. Forget women's magazines.

I avoided Marsalis Zoo and Morrell from Corinth to Marsalis and anywhere in sight of Cliff Temple's high pointy roof. Along a sidewalk, often I saw a head of large spiky black hair from the back, maybe accompanied by a white knee-length skirt tight around the hips. Driving, I'd slow as I passed to watch Gawene's face appear, because those church women were wrong, and the couple customers who had heard of the Stevenses were wrong. When that face came around the hair and it was just flat or had a big chin or heavy brow, I felt a jab. I even went down to Laurel Land, and that steel marker that said "Gawene Areta Stevens" was as wrong as the church women. Gawene was lost somewhere, that was all.

A couple times after I drove past the hair and saw the wrong face, I had to pull over and struggle a while. Later I staggered myself, when I pulled up to a house, I could dry up and wipe off the face and go and joke and jive for a sale and no sooner hit the front walk than the old gates opened again. I walked and climbed into the car in such a way no one in the window could see my eyes. Work kept me on the go that first year, because when I had rest periods, no calls, I'd drive and drive, circling too close to houses and warehouses I shouldn't. Maybe that warehouse nut off Industrial had pulled his revenge when I turned down his clique. Rick Junior might have stomped me for dissing his hot deals. I even drove a few times to Lynnhurst the back route, avoiding Morrell, past the front of the doghouse man's. After all, at Laurel Land Gawene's plate was nested between Tim's and Palla's, all three with the same date, August 28. I don't know what happened to Palla's baby.

But days of full workload, I got so busy dodging traffic, running from one deal to the next and occupying my mind with the gab you had to give to customers, I was connecting one point in the day to the next to get to some end. Then I got to the end, no more calls, watching the cones of my headlights cut through the dark. And something did come, almost every night. Same way I pushed from the bottom of the day and into night, this thing pushed from the bottom of me like a fist and straight out my eyes. This kind of crying I'd never known, it was its own animal. It welled up your eyeballs till they felt ready to break. Then it wrung them, in spasms, five and ten seconds, squeezing the water out, pause, another spasm. It was pulling something out of you, some big worm, and it was spitting that worm out through your eyes. It was telling you over and over, beating your forehead, you'd never again see her, never, never. Then it fell back a couple minutes and dropped you stranded somewhere and went into hiding. Then for a couple minutes the town was its everyday strings of roads and houses and quiet streetlights. But the thing jumped out of hiding and wrung your eyes another hour. Never see her. Never hear her say I know you won't go away. Never watch the way she holds a burger right at the next place on the bun she's about to bite. Never feel her skin wrapped around you. Never see the kid. Never pick her up at work and drive her home.

Your eyes get muscle sore. Sleep comes down.

Sometime when I was sixteen, the full year came and went with no relief, and I got a junk birth certificate and a driver's license.

28.

While I sat in the car watching for Dad, more than Gawene's voice telling me to go talk to him got me fingering my door latch. My own voice said, he might know the facts about the Stevenses. But then he appeared at his door, and my fingers stopped. Three metal plates told me enough facts.

Then one evening in late winter, I pulled into the strip mall and got a wakeup. There was no strip mall.

Across Spanish Fort Road, upright coils of fence wire stood along the street every ten yards. Over the past couple years, I seemed to have floated through haze. I had gone a month without coming to Dad's and missed the whole razing of the strip mall. The last few units at Illinois not boarded up had gotten boarded up. I had heard, without it striking my numb head, how even Rick Ocotillo had packed up. Not one light pushed through a board nailed into a unit. Those coils announced how the police signs posted at Illinois for years had meant business. The police were about to fence off the units and level them as they had the strip mall. Was Dad still in his basement?

His car was gone from its space, and the old orange streetlight above it was out. So were all the orange street lights down the block. In two years, Illinois had blinked out as I watched. I hadn't even spotted Dad for, was it a month, two?

The fence coils kept me late. I even got out of the car, like I rarely do there, and stalked around the parking lot. From the mounds of rubble still waiting to be flattened to a field, behind tumbling-down fence, grumbles came now and then. Lost beamers had made base houses from dirt piles. Spanish Fort Avenue spat up a car only every hour or two, since everything down that way had faded away.

Around eleven, from Illinois the '78 Honda came crawling up Spanish Fort

The car came so slow, even seemed to buck left and right from stomach pains, it'd have to give up its legs any second. The headbeams flickered. At the sight of them still alive, I actually sighed. First time in three and a half years watching for him, I felt relieved to see him.

With no command from me, my feet were going for his parking space. When he was bending over his door to shut it, I stood ten feet off. He stooped so far when he turned to walk he might fall onto his face. Faint light came from Illinois. No more innards appeared to live under the tee shirt.

I came around in front of him. He looked up, had to see me in the light, if his eyes still saw the footpath. But he kept inching along. Under the scant hair and around his eyes, his skull appeared to show through. A bundle sagged under arm.

"Sorry, shop's closed for the night," he said. His first words to his son gone three and a half years. He must have forgotten the missing cash.

"Dad!" I said. "I didn't come to shop."

He kept walking, passed me, and I came along to the door, that is the boards with a door cut through it. Could he hear? He had patched on a new lock. The boards had ax marks. He unlocked and left the door open for me, the only sign he might have recognized me. I was overweight as ever but a couple inches taller. My upper lip and cheeks were sprouting black spider-legs. "Kindly lock the door behind you," he said, and I did.

The stairway was dark as usual. First thing I noticed: he lifted no steel hatch. Maybe he was too weak to lift it anymore. Our feet led the way down the old stairs that groaned and squealed more than ever. But I kept bumping him, he was so slow. My hand hitting his back scared me because that back felt sturdy as a sheet of paper. In the room, I heard him put down the bundle and pat around for matches. I got a whiplash from a new foul odor, above the old stench of half-burned white gas and toasted kokomo. Now the place smelled dampened and buried in the earth for years. But I could not place a new, downright fetid touch. City services had long been cut. From a corner came a noise like a toy ambulance siren. He lit the gas lantern, which huffed. He turned the element to its lowest burn before extinction.

He looked up, from his stoop, had to push upon the counter to see me. He'd let the goatee go to full beard; the hairs looked like a cat had been pawing them. His whole face had collapsed into two canyons plunging down both cheeks. I felt awful, like three and a half years ago I had scraped him out the window as I would too much ketchup off my fries.

I said, "You making out okay? Anybody still around?"

The sound like a toy siren started up again. The place was still crammed as ever, stacks of magazines, boxes of neatly folded clothes, a five-gallon of water on the drainboard. He had to have had that five-gallon delivered. But in one open carton on the floor was a wrapped blanket, and it moved. At first I thought he had a kitten under there, making that siren whine. But then it kept moving, and under the blanket it was bigger and clumsier than a kitten. So that was the new smell, diapers. Dad took a box of dried milk from the bundle he had carried in and shoved his bent back across the room to the open carton.

"He has a few pimples," Dad said, singsongy, like a demented old man, "and he has a big stomach, and he likes to eat a lot, and he wants to eat now."

Closer to the carton, I saw at the end of the rolled blanket a human head. It couldn't have been five, six, seven months old, from the kids I'd seen of customers'. Purple blemishes covered a cheek, the "pimples," I guessed.

Dad poured the milk powder into a baby bottle and at the five-gallon opened the spigot. I was still waiting for a response to my happy "Dad!" on seeing him outside.

I said, "Who's baby? You babysitting?"

"He's not from around here." I took it to mean Dad wasn't babysitting. The baby was far whiter than either of us. His face at least was scrawnier than Dad, and Dad's pants were tents sunken on their poles.

I said, "He's yours? From some woman?" For a second I saw where I might have been about sixteen years ago.

Dad poked the nipple into the lips, and the baby's cheeks pumped so fast the bottle boiled. Dad was paying more attention to this kid than to the one he hadn't seen in ages. Had he always been so off-focus and I hadn't noticed?

"He's mine all right, and he's from some woman all right but no one I know," Dad said. The milk bubbles sounded like a complaining stomach. Dad held the bottle with one hand, left the baby in the box, not even cradling the head or touching the face or coo-cooing. "He's a Gullo, yeah, he has a name all right."

I couldn't see an agency registering an orphan to Dad. Dad was hallucinating. He might have scooped up the baby as someone else might have scooped up Palla Stevens's. I looked around for other milk containers, to gauge how long he'd been carrying on this charade. But Dad at least carried out trash, if not much else. I saw only the usual puzzle mags, electronics parts and stacks of clothes in their baskets, no inventory. The wall hook above the Bible had lost its .38, though, and the Bible had gone, too.

"So," I said, "what you been doing these last years? Business good?"

He watched the kid, with nothing like the wonder I'd seen in parents feeding their babies. He could have been observing a mouse hole. I felt as silly asking how he'd been as he might have felt hearing me ask it. I had been the one to leave. But he showed no flicker that he felt bad himself. He said, "I call him Pricklin. He has these prickling shoots of black hair."

"For real? His name's Pricklin?"

"Real as Gullo. Pricklin Gullo."

"You can't leave him with a name like Pricklin. He has to go to school." I had no place speaking up, considering I was a Chabney. I'd gotten little flack for the name, in a school of Dubals and Kwames. But I wasn't here to squabble about anything I'd carried since infancy. "Why would you take in a kid? You have any guns to sell?"

"Look at him guzzle," Dad said. After a while the kid was done with guzzle and Dad got bored and wandered to his own clear yellow milk on the drainboard. No stems or pipes or kabukis were creeping up out of the furnishings, only the faintest odor of sweet and chemical, so maybe he couldn't even pay for the piedras anymore.

But Dad soon set out on his old pacing about the room anyway, perhaps out of habit, if more stooped and jagged in his path. When I smelled the sudden hot need for diaper change, I poked about for some torn sheets Dad had been using. The lightness under the fabric was what gave me chills. The half-year-olds I'd seen, at least not the boubou starved ones awaiting their own steel marker, looked a good nine or ten pounds. This one couldn't be half that. Dad had done one sensible thing: kept this baby in wraps in the summer. Because when I unwrapped him, he shook like the chills.

The sheet the kid was wearing was loaded with wet. I improvised with pins and clips as I had with many a pistol. I had to keep looking away from that roadkill of a body, skin at the thighs shriveling like an old lady's wrist.

The kid nodded off while Dad became Buddha, though I'd heard Buddha was a quiet prophet. "I'll find the fixin's of mortals in you, I will, right down your throat," he growled at the ceiling. His voice was losing force and getting scratchy. "I'll tell it to everybody, then where'll you be?"

He was making less sense, but it made me happy he kept some old ways. The baby slept well through the ruckus till Dad conked out against a wall.

29.

I stayed that night. Dad on the floor propped against the wall, a baby in a carton five feet away, I couldn't walk out. I'd seen beamers gone thirty days without food, hair falling out till their skull showed green. But they were twenty, twenty-five, skin still had the last glow of baby. Dad, however white he was underneath, was brown and gray as a moldy cigar.

The sight kept me on the chair, picturing what he must have gone through. Just one sell after another, going from cheaper to cheaper, in unit basements between here and Singleton Road. Out of this whole dark complex, his Coleman lantern still breathed, if just above off. Yeah, he must have found this kid when a customer couldn't answer a knock and the door was cracked.

And the sight of the stacks of magazines and clothes and boxes, the rotten wet home smell despite the rank fresh diaper-odor, all felt good. I had been gone a while, is all, sleeping too much in my car.

My fold-out mattress was missing from the closet. I laid out a bed of clothes on the last bare patch of carpet. The basement was cooler than outside even in summers and cool enough nights to leave the damp floor clammy. With the old pole, I lowered the steel hatch, then turned the lantern valve so the gas hiss petered out. The element shined bright a second more and shivered from its own hot air and died out.

Dreams kept my eyes so busy, I'd stir and the eyeballs were twirling.

The kid's mewling woke me to a basement empty of Dad.

I lit the lantern, and the steel hatch was open. Enough morning air came down to cool. On the kid, what I had thought were pimples were something big, purple and crying. I could use a doctor.

I made a bottle. Under the blanket, the kid wore only some kind of tee, to his feet. The shirt had an iron-on of a cartoon dinosaur. I poked through the damp cardboard boxes in the closet for socks and another old tee-shirt from when I was six, now gray with mildew.

The kid stared at you when you dressed him or fed him or gave the slightest friendly coo. If you touched the sores, he jerked the stare away. But he said little now he was fed and just lay on his back looking at the ceiling. He didn't appear bored but waiting to recover from being too skinny. I told myself, if anything I should stay on a while to pump him with milk till he filled out. Maybe someone had done the same for me some years ago.

I took the old wood chair with the lathed poles up the back that gnawed even into my padded ribs. We had salvaged it from a moved-out family's pile next door when I was seven. So here I was at home. It had seemed all of three and a half years ago. Even the insides looked three and a half years worn. One stack of catalogs, towels, gift boxes and racks of planter pots had not moved since last seen. But it appeared about ten inches shorter, sunken with gravity and damp. The place was silent as the kid. No Rick Ocotillo up yakking at residents, no codes knuckling the outside door. Only the kid's nose breath, something new, and leaves rolling in the breeze beyond the window. My cough, miracle, slept through the morning. But the leaks through the bricked-in window let that crawly feeling of bumbled codes back into my gut. I squirmed out of the chair and paced.

The kid drained two more bottles of milk before Dad returned early afternoon. The key rattling the upstairs lock jolted me to run cover the kid, as if wool could stop buckshot. But I could tell Dad's feeble way of twisting the key a dozen times left and right in a slot. He appeared at the open hatch. He shook his head as he dropped both feet onto one stairstep at a time. "It's Saturday, so the fence ain't growing."

"It will Monday. They can do it in a day."

No bundles under arm explained where he'd been. He inched to the chair, dropped in it and blinked some exhausted eyes.

"You got a place set up?" I said. "You got this kid, you don't want to be stuck inside this fence." Dad did not appear like he could climb it, much less with a kid in a backpack.

"That's like the City, begin a project on Friday in time to pause for the weekend."

I was standing a good eight feet off. When his eyes settled on me a couple seconds they felt like the gouged-out ones at the taxidermist's when I'd come to sell. "Dad, you remember I left you that February? You notice I been gone a while?"

His gaze didn't jump but just stared into one nothing a few seconds, then drifted into another nothing. Boubou had done a good wipedown. Dad had always talked at you, but now he was leaving out the you to talk at.

He actually glanced at the baby. "Come Monday or Tuesday, I may have to have my car out before it's fenced in."

Then will he move on? He'd no more say than he'd say what he's been doing for a living or why he ever left airplane mechanics.

"The kid's underweight," I said.

"Rick Ocotillo sold us out. To the City. They say he's living in San Antonio on a pension, if he isn't dead. Me and Millard Foreman up in 23R are the last to stick it out."

Dad was living in another age, because no one but him and the breeze remained at Illinois.

He went on, "He changes units every night, so I can't find him."

I had no patience anymore to answer a head like his. When I came inside last night, I'd thought I had patience.

"But this fence takes everything from everybody," he said.

"So where you going?"

He shook his head a moment till it came to a stop.

Dad did have some of the usual food, potato flakes and fried pork skins, and we gathered them into a meal. He was too out of joint to shoplift, so money had to come somehow. I snorted a lot of potatoes and skins and felt bad for the freeload. But this battleship needed fuel to escort this baby dinghy to shore. I could not speak for the broken canoe.

For one thing, that broken canoe managed to get around: After dinner I dozed off in that stuffy place and woke around dawn to find him disappeared again. He liked to sneak out under the noise of my snores. The kid was yowling with a terror of a haunted cat. No surprise; he'd made it a whole night without a peep for drink. I knocked around for its bottle, and the milk powder was rattling hollow in the box. It's like that death scream was hearing the end of rations. The rate he was wolfing, he had maybe twenty-four hours left in the box. I hoped Dad was Sunday shopping.

The bottle alone didn't quiet the racket. I took the bundle of blankets in arm. It was so light, that bundle, so horribly light, I lost control. It just blew out of me in the same way Gawene's death would blow out of me when I drove down the street. It came out in spasms. I just held onto that bundle, probably too tight, as if I could give it some of my flesh. It was a bundle of air. I stuck my cheek to his, that tissue paper cheek.

I washed the bubbles on the baby's face many times. It seemed to help dry them, and by evening they were shrinking some.

My car, I kept thinking, stayed exposed on the parking lot. It didn't have a bad-looking skin itself, so it made a good pick. I tried to picture it was okay, the green tinted windshield still clear, and picture how the countryside looked past the city. There had to be the kinds of small towns you see on television, with the square in the middle and the old men who run dusty stores. One of them would need help, and if I had a kid in tow they would never guess I'd once sold guns without a license. But also I'd never driven out of the city.

Dad returned late, keeping his day secret again. He shared a can of dinner.

"Pricklin's about run out of milk," I said, "and he has diarrhea."

"Tomorrow's Monday. City's going to return to work."

He was gone when Pricklin woke me early.

30.

I went upstairs with Pricklin. I had to find him a new name.

Standing at the outside door with the kid in arms, I looked out on the workers. Past them, on the wide parking lot, miracle, my car remained, whether or not the engine did. Along Spanish Fort, two men dug postholes with a power digger, about five minutes a hole. They moved up twenty feet for the next. A cement truck followed and shot a wad into the hole. Guys came with fence posts. Coils of fence wire waited. It was a slapdash operation, probably invented by the cops just for Illinois. The complex couldn't be a thousand feet long, a couple hundred wide. At this rate, the men could have the place fenced by tonight.

In the basement, the kid—I was starting to think of him as Suds—killed the last of the milk. He demanded to be held, then squirmed in my arms like he smelled the milk box was empty. I tried the juice from canned fruit cocktail, which he inhaled, juice from canned beans, which he grabbed with both arms. I wished I'd babysat once before.

Dad stayed out all day. As I stood in the outside door, that coil seemed to unwind faster than the men walked. I tried to picture hoisting a baby over an eight-foot fence, alone, without breaking anyone's spine. I mean, I had not lost that much weight on two days of potato flakes. But how could I leave Dad? How could I do it to him again?

More like, who could let him do anything to anyone again.

City Limit

I hurried with Suds to the opposite side of the complex, where the last few posts were still bare of fence wire. We walked the long way around the fence to the strip mall lot, and beyond the fence we saw Dad's empty parking space and his open apartment door.

We sat in my driver's seat. You were in my lap. Who had booster seats? Your head was about an inch from the wheel. I turned the ignition, and the engine proved it still existed, with a good shout. You, now, the morning was warm, but still I had to keep that wrap from twirling off your paperclip toes, you, now, on hearing that big engine, went right to sleep.

Lantzey Miller has worked in landscaping, restaurant kitchens and counters, a research laboratory, and industrial supplies and took a master's degree and then taught classes. He prefers food, trees, the company of non-adults, real objects, solitude, acoustic instruments and dance and song. He is at work on his next two novels.